About t

Damon L. Wakes was born in 1991 and began to write a few years later. He holds an MA in Creative and Critical Writing from the University of Winchester, and a BA in English Literature from the University of Reading.

When he isn't writing, Damon enjoys weaving chainmail and making jewellery. He produces items made of modern metals such as aluminium, niobium and titanium, but constructed using thousand-year-old techniques.

Damon's other interests are diverse. He has at various times taken up archery, fencing and kayaking, ostensibly as research for books but mostly because it's something to do.

TEN LITTLE ASTRONAUTS

TEN LITTLE
ASTRONAUTS

DAMON L. WAKES

Damon L.
Wakes

Unbound Digital

This edition first published in 2018

Unbound

6th Floor Mutual House, 70 Conduit Street, London W1S 2GF

www.unbound.com

All rights reserved

© Damon L. Wakes, 2018

The right of Damon L. Wakes to be identified as the author of this work has been asserted in accordance with Section 77 of the Copyright, Designs and Patents Act 1988. No part of this publication may be copied, reproduced, stored in a retrieval system, or transmitted, in any form or by any means without the prior permission of the publisher, nor be otherwise circulated in any form of binding or cover other than that in which it is published and without a similar condition being imposed on the subsequent purchaser.

This book is a work of fiction and, except in the case of historical fact, any resemblance to actual persons, living or dead, is purely coincidental.

ISBN (eBook): 978-1-912618-67-5
ISBN (Paperback): 978-1-912618-66-8

Cover design by Mecob

Printed and bound in Great Britain by Clays Ltd, Elcograf S.p.A.

In memory of William Craig: gentleman, scholar, and orator.

Dear Reader,

The book you are holding came about in a rather different way to most others. It was funded directly by readers through a new website: Unbound.

Unbound is the creation of three writers. We started the company because we believed there had to be a better deal for both writers and readers. On the Unbound website, authors share the ideas for the books they want to write directly with readers. If enough of you support the book by pledging for it in advance, we produce a beautifully bound special subscribers' edition and distribute a regular edition and e-book wherever books are sold, in shops and online.

This new way of publishing is actually a very old idea (Samuel Johnson funded his dictionary this way). We're just using the internet to build each writer a network of patrons. At the back of this book, you'll find the names of all the people who made it happen.

Publishing in this way means readers are no longer just passive consumers of the books they buy, and authors are free to write the books they really want. They get a much fairer return too – half the profits their books generate, rather than a tiny percentage of the cover price.

If you're not yet a subscriber, we hope that you'll want to join our publishing revolution and have your name listed in one of our books in the future. To get you started, here is a £5 discount on your first pledge. Just visit unbound.com, make your pledge and type ASTRO18 in the promo code box when you check out.

Thank you for your support,

Dan, Justin and John
Founders, Unbound

Eleven

Even before the alarm began to sound, Blair knew in his gut that something was wrong. It was only when he pushed open the hatch of the suspension tank, and a few drops of thick cryonic fluid drifted out into the pitch-black hallway, that he realised what it was: there was no gravity. That was why his stomach churned. The world, the tiny pool of light spilling from his tank, seemed to swirl.

'Owen, lights.'

The computer gave no response.

'Owen, turn on the lights.'

Nothing.

'Owen...' But there was something else now, beyond the cold tank and the dark hallway. Something that no crewman wanted to encounter anywhere, let alone ten trillion kilometres beyond Earth orbit.

It was the smell of burning plastic.

Blair hauled himself out of the tank and clawed for the rack of emergency supplies. Even the smallest fire could render the air unbreathable very quickly. Finally managing to find a torch, he tore it from its bracket and pumped the dynamo. A feeble light flickered into life.

Without gravity, every direction was downwards. Away from the wall of suspension tanks and handrails, the darkness of the hallway yawned like an endless chasm. Gradually the smell of scorched plastic grew stronger. The end of the passage loomed in the torchlight, and Blair pulled himself hand over hand towards the steel door of Computing Hub Five. He heaved it open, and the torch picked out a blizzard of extinguisher foam. Someone else was already here. Sweeping the torch across the room, he spotted a figure in the far corner, clutching an extinguisher, but the man hung motionless in the air. A ball of blood was forming on his back, held by surface tension to the axe planted between his ribs. A constellation of droplets spread throughout the room.

Blair fought back the urge to cry for help. This man was dead, and there was every chance that whoever had killed him was still nearby. The clumps of foam suspended in mid-air drifted slowly through the beam of the torch, casting shadows that slunk and flickered across the banks of equipment lining the room.

'In the event of an emergency, the ship defrosts ten crew members.'

Blair wheeled round to see a black-haired man, and a small group behind him, clinging to the handrails at the doorway to the next cryonic bay.

'With you and your friend over there,' the man continued, gesturing to the corpse, 'I make that eleven.'

Ten

A large man in a blue security jumpsuit shifted his position, feet braced against a wall rail, ready to leap. He had the sort of face – unusually flat and decidedly asymmetrical – that suggested he had at some point broken his nose. He had the sort of knuckles that suggested he might also have broken someone else's.

Blair remained perfectly still. 'I'm an engineer,' he explained, as calmly as he could. 'My biometrics are on file, and I intend to cooperate fully.'

'You can start by passing over that torch.' The security officer stretched out a massive hand. 'Slowly.'

Blair let go of the torch and shoved it gently towards him. The off-centre mass of the battery and dynamo caused it to spin as it drifted, the beam sweeping through the mist of blood and foam that filled the room.

The security officer snatched it from the air. Blair suddenly found the light focused on him, dazzling him. Disoriented, he gripped the door frame with both hands.

'If it was him,' the first man spoke again, 'he did a remarkably neat job.'

Blair looked at his jumpsuit, and to his horror realised it was spattered with blood. But then, so was everyone else's.

The security officer snapped the plastic body of the torch forwards, converting it into a rudimentary lantern. 'This way.' He gestured to the corridor. 'Best close off this room.'

Following the spots in his vision, Blair pulled himself along the wall of the room and into the corridor, following the others. He slid the door shut before joining the group: five on one wall, five on the other. Blair didn't recognise any of them. There were four thousand people frozen on board the *Owen*; he knew maybe forty.

The security officer held the lantern out in the middle of the corridor, then slowly drew his hand away, leaving it suspended in mid-air.

The group watched him, waiting. Whether by agreement or his own natural authority, he commanded their respect.

'Alright.' The flat-nosed officer let out a long breath. 'My name is Lawson Warwick: at present the only security officer available to respond to this crime. As I see it, there are two possibilities here. Either we have a stowaway, or the ship defrosted an extra person. It seems to me that the simplest way of identifying anyone who isn't supposed to be here would be to identify everyone who is. I want to know everybody's name, position, and anything that could help confirm that information.'

'Fine.' The response was immediate. 'I'll start.'

Blair looked at the man who had spoken. Where others clung fearfully to the handrail, his fingers were barely closed around it: the stars were home to him.

The man stared back around the group. 'My name is Edmund Aldrin. I'm one of the engineers assigned to central networking. I can't tell you anything to back that up but I can tell you this: if we don't get the mainframe back online then the stowaway will be the least of our problems.'

'Alright.' Warwick nodded at the next person along. 'Now you.'

'I'm not finished.' Aldrin grabbed hold of a rail on the ceiling, pulling himself into the centre of the group. 'I don't give a damn who you are or what you do. I can get the computer running again, but to do that I've got to go outside the ship. The mainframe runs hot: it's in the central fuselage, separated from the cryonic bays by a quarter-kilometre crawl through open space. Naturally I'll need a little help from in here.'

Aldrin looked about the group. There was a nod from a grey-haired man near Blair, but no response from anybody else.

'We can't afford to be hasty here.' Warwick shook his head. 'If we take the time to get all the facts, there's a chance we can resolve this here and now.'

'If I can get to the mainframe, there'll be nothing to resolve. We can just check the ship's records and be done with it. Who's with me?'

A thin, angular woman and a pale-looking man moved forward to join him. Blair considered it as well: restarting the mainframe would likely involve little more than resetting a few breakers. But what if Aldrin demanded assistance? What if Blair himself was asked to clamber out into the blank expanse of space?

Sensing Blair's indecision, Aldrin addressed him. 'What about you?'

Blair hesitated. 'We don't know how long it'll take to get the computer running, or how long this bay will remain habitable: the neighbouring bays are still at maybe six Kelvin, and they're leaching heat from ours. Somebody needs to start the backup generators and get life support online.'

'Navigation, too,' a short woman nearby broke in. 'We were due to accelerate constantly for the first half of the journey, then decelerate for the rest of it. If we drift past the halfway point while the computer's down – or if we're past it already – we could overshoot our destination. If that happens, there's no way back.'

A loud creak echoed through the ship, the hull shifting and contracting as the air inside cooled. Blair was suddenly very conscious of the yawning void just beyond those walls.

'Oh no.' A portly man with a moustache gripped the rail with both hands, pulling himself against the wall. His eyes were squeezed shut. 'Oh, please no.'

Warwick held up a hand, weighty as a judge's gavel. 'If we could just take a minute—'

'Why?' asked the grey-haired man. 'Why are you so determined that we wait?'

Warwick looked at Aldrin. 'I don't think any of us knows anyone else here. You're entrusting your life to these people and you have no idea who they are.'

'I know that these three are trying to help, which is more than I can say for you.'

Warwick opened his mouth, but didn't speak. The eyes of the group were upon him.

The black-haired man spoke. 'I must say, I'm with Officer Warwick.'

'Thank you,' said Warwick. 'I'm glad to hear it, Mister…'

'Lambert.' He put out a well manicured hand to shake. 'Felix Lambert. I'm a logistics manager for the U.N. *Owen*. I can't say I was prepared for this situation, but I've got a fair idea what sort of crew members the ship would select to respond to a crisis and if there's any chance I can spot the odd one out then I think I should try.'

'Go ahead.' Aldrin pushed off from the rail and drifted over to a nearby storeroom. 'If you get anywhere with that, let us know.' He reached inside and produced a portable radio, which he shoved towards Lambert.

Lambert caught it. Aldrin selected more items from the storeroom – tools, a small generator, a pair of magnetic anchors – and his followers moved over to help with the equipment.

Nobody said anything for a moment. The whole situation felt unreal. Blair half expected to find himself back in the suspension tank, to discover this whole ordeal no more than a hallucination, a consequence of being flash-thawed.

'Well, Lambert and I have introduced ourselves.' Warwick looked at Blair. 'What about you?'

'I'm, ah, Wilson Blair. Another engineer.' He tried to think if there was anything else to add. Anything that would help gain the trust of the group after he'd been found in the room with the murdered man. There wasn't.

Warwick didn't demand anything more, instead nodding at the short woman next to him.

'Eva Roberts,' she said. 'Navigation officer.' Her tone was crisp, smart, professional.

Aldrin and his three followers left through a hatch in the ceiling, heading for the airlock. The others watched them go, then looked at the young woman next to Roberts.

'Verna Clements. Flight technician.' She took a breath, as though to add some other detail, but it never came. She, like Blair, had no proof to offer.

Only the man with the moustache was left, but he remained silent, clinging to the wall. Though the situation had everyone ill at ease, he was evidently struggling to cope. The group waited respectfully for him to speak, but still he did not, and the sympathy Blair had felt at first soon changed to suspicion.

Lambert placed a hand on the man's shoulder. 'Come now. We'll get through this, Mister...'

The man blinked a few times, then brought up a hand to sweep away the tears that had nowhere to fall. 'McConnell. My name's McConnell.'

'And how about you tell us what you do on board the *Owen*?'

His face hardened. 'My position is classified.'

Everybody was stunned.

Warwick fixed him with a stare. 'Surely you realise how suspicious that sounds.'

'I do.' McConnell glanced warily at the five faces surrounding him. 'But once you get the computer working, checking my identity will be trivial. If I were to reveal any sensitive information before then... the board of directors would not be pleased. It could cause me a great deal of bother.'

'I should think you might encounter more bother if you don't,' said Warwick, his tone dangerously polite.

McConnell's jowls quivered. 'I won't be threatened,' he said, still gripping the handrail. 'But I hope you'll appreciate that, were I trying to deceive you, I would have offered a far more convincing story.'

Lambert rubbed a hand across his jaw. 'Besides our "classified" Mister McConnell, we seem to make up a fairly typical emergency response team. Though I can't comment on the three who went with Aldrin.'

Blair hadn't expected much more. With their small group divided, the whole endeavour already felt futile. 'We should sort out life support. At the very least it'll buy us more time to deal with everything else.'

'No.' All eyes were on Roberts. She may have been small, but she clearly wasn't afraid to speak her mind. 'We need to restore navigation. There are four thousand people on board this ship, and they're depending on us to get them though the journey. Everything – even our own lives – comes second to that.'

Blair stared at Roberts in surprise. So did the others.

'It won't come to that,' said Warwick, firmly.

Roberts met his gaze with a schoolteacher's frown. 'I hope not. But we can't take any chances. There's no way of knowing how long we've been travelling, or what speed the ship's reached.'

Blair looked about the bare metal hallway, its unlit walls. His eyes fell upon a thick glass tube bolted over the doorway to Hub Five. 'There is one way,' he said.

The others watched as Blair pushed himself over to the door.

He pointed out the tube. 'The tritium in these door markers has a half-life of just over twelve years, but they're not giving off any light any more.' He turned back to the group. 'We've been frozen for more than thirty years. Possibly a lot more.'

Thirty years of constant acceleration. Though the ship felt motionless, they had likely travelled thousands of kilometres in the time he'd taken to reach the door.

Roberts' lips were a thin, hard line. 'I'm heading to navigation. The rest of you can do what you like.'

'Wait.' Warwick held up a hand. 'I don't like this. I don't think we should split up, under the circumstances.'

'You don't have to like it.' Roberts tugged herself over to the next handrail along. 'But it's happening.'

'Then we form two groups. There are six of us: three go to life support, three to navigation. That way everybody has someone to watch their back.'

Roberts paused. She turned to Clements. 'You said you were a flight technician?'

Clements hesitated before answering. 'That's right.' Her voice was quiet.

'You're with me.' Roberts moved over to the storeroom and retrieved a small toolkit.

Clements followed meekly, her hands and feet barely making a sound on the rails. Blair wondered if this was her first time out of orbit: she seemed comfortable enough without gravity, but showed none of the same confidence as Aldrin or Roberts.

Blair looked at McConnell, who in turn looked at Warwick. McConnell pulled at his moustache with a pudgy hand, some thought heavy on his mind. 'I'm coming too,' he said, throwing himself unsteadily towards Roberts and Clements. It wasn't the response Blair had expected.

'I should think not!' Warwick made a grab for his ankle, but missed. 'You think I'd leave you alone with two women?'

'Excuse me?' Roberts glared at Warwick. 'I'm sure these two women will be more than capable of dealing with him if we have to.'

Clements looked less sure, but said nothing.

'And besides,' she ducked back into the storeroom, 'we've got a radio. You can reach us if you get in trouble.'

Warwick frowned, but didn't argue. 'The signal won't carry far in here,' he said. 'Nobody close any doors.'

Roberts, Clements and McConnell took their equipment and left. Blair looked at Warwick, then Lambert. They weren't a bad pair to be with, he considered. Warwick's blue jumpsuit would have been a strange choice for a stowaway trying to blend in, and it made sense that the ship would have defrosted at least one security officer. Similarly, though there was nothing to set Lambert apart in terms of appearance, his familiarity with the ship suggested he was meant to be on board.

Blair spoke to them: 'We'd best go this way.' He gestured to the opposite end of the corridor, away from Computing Hub Five. 'Probably best not to disturb… you know.'

'Just a moment.' Warwick spoke quietly enough to be sure his voice would not carry to either of the other groups. 'If you can stomach it, I'd like another look in there. Without all the others gaggling round.'

'What's this about?' demanded Lambert.

'I want another look at the body. Someone in this bay is a murderer, and the contents of that room are our best chance of finding out who.' He turned to Blair. 'You said we could afford to look after ourselves if it bought us more time to patch up the ship?'

'Something like that.' Blair glanced at the door.

'Well I should say we'd all work a lot faster if we didn't have to keep watching over our shoulders. Don't you agree?'

Blair and Lambert had to concede that they would.

'Right then.' Warwick pushed off towards the door of Computing Hub Five, braced his feet against the wall, and slid it partway open.

A haze of thin smoke wafted out into the corridor. A curl of extinguisher foam, tinged red with blood, stretched around the door frame like the tendril of some strange anemone. It seemed to clutch at Warwick's elbow as he slipped inside.

Taking a deep breath of the comparatively clean air of the hallway, Blair followed with the light. The inside of the computing hub was unnaturally quiet. He could hear no snapping of relays, no hum of coolant pumps. The ship was a dead tin can.

Warwick pulled himself towards the body, still floating in the far corner of the room. He paused to examine the thick cables bolted to the wall.

'Blair,' he called, 'you might want to have a look at this.'

Blair joined him. Lambert followed.

'What do you make of that?'

There was a burnt-out notch carved into the cables. It wasn't hard to imagine what had caused it. 'Someone's put an axe through the main power and networking cables. The current must have run through the axe head from one into the other. That's what's fried...' he swung the torch across the room, 'everything, really.'

'And probably why this chap here had to go for the fire extinguisher,' put in Lambert.

Warwick moved over to inspect the axe, still lodged in the corpse's back. Fighting his revulsion, Blair brought the light over to the body.

Warwick blew forcefully on the blood collected around the axe head – already starting to congeal – to disperse it. The droplets hit the nearby wall and scattered. The non-slip plastic coating near the head of the axe was scorched and melted, the steel beneath heat anodised to a bronze sheen.

'This is the axe that did it.' Warwick put a hand out for the torch, and Blair passed it over. Warwick directed the beam about the room. 'He came in over there.' The far doorway, its extinguisher bracket empty. 'He doused the equipment.' The smouldering computer terminal, caked with foam. 'The killer was already in the room.' The narrow space between two computer banks. 'Whoever it was probably struck once the air was full of foam. This chap never even knew they were here.'

Warwick's sequence of events didn't do anything to shed light on the identity of the killer, but it did make one thing absolutely clear: this had been an ambush. Whoever had snuck on board had chosen to hide here after cutting the cables, and they had chosen to murder the first crew member to appear. Blair shuddered. He had come through that very same doorway, would have gone for that very same extinguisher if it hadn't already been used. It could so easily have been him.

The radio crackled, fragments of speech drifting through. Lambert lifted the device to his ear. 'I can't make anything out,' he said.

'Take it to the door!' Blair pushed off from the wall as hard as he could. He hurtled through the air, catching hold of a handrail near the door frame. The force of the impact jarred his elbows, but he didn't slow down. If someone was using their radio this soon after the group had split up, there was a good chance that the killer had struck again. Pressing his feet against the door, he slid it all the way open. Lambert, only a second behind him, darted through into the corridor beyond.

The radio began to pick up the faint signal: '... not sure what... do. We need... airlock open, but... shouldn't be...' It was Aldrin.

Eva Roberts' voice came in. 'Can you tell how it got there? Has it been attached since launch?'

'I don't know. Seems like Lambert would be the one to ask, but he's gone quiet. You don't think...'

Lambert pressed the transmit button. 'I'm here. Just had a little radio trouble. What's going on?'

'There's a ship docked,' explained Aldrin. 'Looks to be a small craft, just one suspension tank, the sort of thing used to shift mining equipment around the asteroid belt. Whoever's here, whoever's on board, this is how they got in.'

Warwick shoved through the doorway and held out a hand for the mouthpiece of the radio. Lambert hesitated, then passed it over.

'Who knows about this?' demanded Warwick.

'Everyone.' There was a note of triumph in Aldrin's voice.

'Right. I want everybody back at the computing hub now. That ship is our best chance of identifying our intruder. I want it to remain sealed until I can conduct a proper search. Nobody is to go in there.'

There was a whispered argument at the other end, chopped up by bursts of static. It sounded as though more than one person had their hands on the mouthpiece.

The next man's voice to come over the radio, Blair didn't recognise. 'So only you get to see inside that ship?'

Warwick paused before answering. 'As the only security officer on duty, I am the only person qualified to do so. The more of us who enter, the more chance there is that somebody will destroy vital evidence.'

'Does that not seem awfully convenient to everyone?'

Warwick had been against Aldrin's plan from the start. He'd been awfully keen to get back inside the computing hub, and he'd insisted on doing it without the rest of the group. Suddenly presented with this new turn of events, Blair couldn't help but wonder if Warwick might not be more interested in concealing evidence than collecting it.

Warwick began to clamber along the wall towards the hatch Aldrin's team had gone through. Blair and Lambert followed.

'Processing a crime scene in zero gravity is extremely difficult,' stressed Warwick. 'Every person inside that room will contaminate it. They'll be shedding hair and skin, and it'll drift about so that we can't work out if it was left before the ship docked or after we got inside.'

'What difference will that make?' It was McConnell who spoke this time, from the group working on the navigation system. 'You can't run a DNA test until we get the computer running.'

'Maybe not,' said Warwick, 'but I can check for fingerprints the old-fashioned way if I have to. All I'd need would be some electrical tape and fine powder.'

'And for us to trust you,' put in the man from Aldrin's group. 'Who's to say there isn't a weapon stashed away in there?'

'If there was a weapon in there, why would the murderer have used the axe in the computing hub?' Warwick didn't speak into the mouthpiece. He shouted through the hatch in the ceiling.

'Warwick is the murderer!' the man was shouting too. His voice on the radio, distorted by the volume, was accompanied by an echo through the corridors of the ship. 'Somebody grab him!'

Warwick looked warily at Blair and Lambert. They merely looked back.

Lambert took hold of the radio. 'Let's sort this out, alright?' he said, into the mouthpiece. 'Let's all just take a minute and sort this out.'

'Quite right.' Warwick took hold of the ladder leading towards the airlock and began to climb. 'We can't afford to all turn on one another. I won't have this turning into a witch-hunt.'

Blair followed him.

'Listen to me.' Aldrin was on the radio again. 'We've worked it out. All our jumpsuits were given to us when we boarded, but the security ones were being used long before launch. I don't know if he was stationed at the launch platform or just stole a uniform from someone who was, but you can be sure there's a reason he's so determined to stop us going in that ship!'

Warwick pushed himself through the hatch, drifting to catch hold of a rail on the ceiling. Blair prepared to follow.

'Stop right there!'

Blair recognised the voice: it was the same man who had shouted over the radio. Illuminated by Warwick's light, he waited at the end of the corridor, a magnetic anchor clutched in his hand. A ragged trail of wires floated near his wrist, tethered to the device. He'd modified it somehow.

'What is this?' shouted Warwick. 'What's going on?'

It was then that Blair spotted the screwdriver resting just behind the anchor's magnetic coil. He grabbed Warwick's ankle. 'Don't move.'

The man nodded at Blair. 'You've seen this trick before, haven't you?'

Warwick looked at him.

'He's made a gun,' Blair explained. 'Those anchors are supposed to keep astronauts attached magnetically to the outside of the ship. But if you put a small metal object near the coil before you turn it on, it'll get pulled out the front with some force.'

'Ordinarily it would barely dent a tin can,' said the man, 'but us electronics boys got playing with them back in orbit. Wire in a capacitor from an arc welder and suddenly it packs quite a punch.'

'And you were worried there might be a weapon on that ship,' sneered Warwick.

'Now, now.' The electrician kept him firmly in his sights. 'If I wanted to shoot you, I'd have done it by now.'

There was a clang of metal on metal, and the ladder shook faintly. Blair chanced a look down and saw the radio drifting below. He looked back at the magnetic anchor, at the screwdriver poised behind the coil, at the man who waited to direct it. His wrinkled eyes were wide with fear, but his hand was steady.

Blair tightened his grip on Warwick's ankle, his suspicions edging towards certainty.

Lambert called up from the bottom of the ladder: 'Listen, if we're putting someone on trial here, I think we should all be around to have our say.'

'There'll be time for that just as soon as the others have had a chance to look inside that s—'

There was a deafening bang, and a sudden blast of wind rushed through the corridor. For just an instant, the narrow hatch at the end of the ladder was like the jet from a power washer. Still clinging to Warwick, Blair found himself floating in the middle of the corridor, struggling to manoeuvre himself into any position where he could catch hold of something solid. His ears were pounding. His lungs ached.

The beam of Warwick's light, spinning uselessly in midair, swung across the corridor. Blair caught sight of several fluorescent canisters protruding from the wall, transparent face masks on tubes stretching out from each one. The beam swung on, revealing that the end of the corridor was now a wall of steel. Something had gone wrong with the airlock. The ship had lost pressure, and the mechanical failsafe had sealed off that section. It was the only reason Blair was still alive.

In the corner of the corridor, the man's hand had been pinned in place by the slamming pressure door, his improvised weapon still pointed towards Warwick. But the rest of him was on the other side. The rest of him was with the others.

Aldrin's team was dead.

Six

Blair was light-headed. He gasped for breath, but the air did nothing to feed his starving lungs. One of the face masks brushed past his fingertip. He snatched for it in the dark and missed. Pushing off from Warwick's thrashing leg, he drifted feebly towards what he hoped was the wall, arms outstretched, straining to reach some kind of handhold. The beam of the light came back around, and he saw that the oxygen mask was well wide of where he thought it had been. He snatched it up and took a few deep breaths.

Nothing.

Blair began to panic. This canister was defective. The mechanism had jammed. In the years he had spent frozen, the casing had corroded and its contents spoiled. He shook it furiously: a last, desperate attempt to trigger the reaction as he fought to remain conscious.

The beam swung past one more time, and Blair spotted the toggle on top of the canister. He ripped it off. There was a snap as the firing pin struck the percussion cap and the sodium chlorate in the canister began to burn, feeding oxygen to the mask. Blair fitted it to his face and stretched the elastic strap back over his head. He allowed himself a moment just to drift, to breathe, to let the dizziness fade.

The light illuminated Warwick, floating motionless by the wall. His breathing was rapid and shallow: he hadn't managed to get a mask on.

Blair kicked over to him, picking up the torch on the way, and pulled the toggle of one of the oxygen generators nearby. He brought the mask over to Warwick's face, held it ready above the flat nose and brutish jaw, but hesitated before fixing it on.

'You're wondering...' Lambert had appeared at the ladder hatch. His mask was already fitted, but he still seemed to be suffering from the thin air. 'Wondering if... it was him.'

Blair pressed the mask over Warwick's nose and mouth and secured it with the elastic strap. 'Yeah,' he said. 'But what if it wasn't?'

The hull creaked and groaned. A fine haze of dust hung suspended in the corridor, brought out by the rush of air through the ship.

Blair shuddered, and it wasn't just fear. 'That breach dropped the temperature in here.' If it hadn't been for the mask, he would have been able to see his breath. 'We need to get life support online. I don't know how long we have.'

'What about Warwick?'

He was still unconscious, but the oxygen would bring him round. If not, there was nothing else they could do.

'Drag him through to life support. I'll catch up.'

Blair grabbed the back of Warwick's collar and shoved him towards Lambert. Too late, he realised that Warwick's oxygen generator was still trailing behind and would tug the mask off his face. Blair reached out and gave it a push.

'Aah!' The metal was already searing hot from the reaction inside. 'Mind the canister!' he warned Lambert. 'Get it by the handle!'

Carefully, Lambert took hold of the canister and began to squirm back through the ladder hatch, pulling Warwick behind him. Instead of following, Blair made his way over to the pressure door and tugged the magnetic anchor from the electrician's dead hand, trying not to look at the place where the flesh of the wrist met the metal of the pressure door. The anchor and its bundle of scavenged electronics was a bulky thing to carry, particularly along with the oxygen generator, but Blair couldn't afford to leave it behind. If Warwick really was the murderer, this makeshift weapon might be the only way of keeping him at bay. Even if he wasn't, Blair certainly wasn't going to leave it behind for anyone else to pick up.

Through the hatch and down the ladder, flecks of dry blood and extinguisher foam drifted through the corridor, drawn out of Hub Five by the decompression. Blair wished they'd thought to shut the door after they'd passed through. Lambert was waiting with Warwick at the opposite end of the corridor, away from the worst of it.

'He started stirring halfway down the ladder. Almost couldn't get him through.' Lambert lifted his oxygen generator. 'Frightfully difficult not to burn yourself on these things.'

'We'll be glad of the heat before too long,' said Blair. He looked around at the row of oxygen generators on either side of the hallway.

They'd have been deployed anywhere the pressure in the ship had dropped too low.

Lambert spoke: 'Do you think Roberts' group is alright?'

'Chances are they're doing better than us.' Blair nodded at a nearby pressure door. 'Since our section's been sealed off, theirs might still have a proper atmosphere.'

The creaking of the hull was joined momentarily by the rapid knocking of a pipe under strain.

'Any idea what went wrong?' asked Lambert, after the noise died down.

Blair shook his head. 'Maybe there was already a breach in the other ship. Maybe it wasn't docked properly. Who knows?'

Blair caught sight of the radio, floating aimlessly. He grabbed the mouthpiece.

'Hello?' he found himself almost shouting into the microphone. 'Hello? Anybody?'

There was no response.

'Maybe we could bring it to a door or something,' Lambert suggested.

Blair grimaced. 'Wouldn't matter if we did. The doors closed because we started losing atmosphere. They won't open until we replace it.'

'How do we fix this?'

It was Warwick who'd spoken. Blair checked the screwdriver was still in place behind the coil of the magnetic anchor.

With nothing to push off against, Warwick made a series of ungainly swings with his arm to bring himself within reach of a handhold. He caught sight of Blair's weapon and gave an irritated sigh. 'Please. It was that fool's paranoia that got us into this mess. The last thing we need now is a repeat of that standoff.'

'The last thing we need now,' said Blair, keeping the device levelled at Warwick's chest, 'is another death.'

'The ship is freezing. The air's too thin to breathe.' Warwick let go of the handhold momentarily and spread his arms. 'If there's going to be another death now it'll be because we don't sort this out!'

'He's right.' Lambert looked at Blair. 'All we can do is take care of our job and hope the other lot take care of theirs.'

It was true, but still Blair didn't take his eyes off Warwick. 'It wasn't just that one man who didn't trust you,' he said. 'If the rest of Aldrin's group didn't agree with him, do you really think they would have let him have a weapon? Let him threaten you – us? Tried to board that ship themselves?'

Lambert said nothing.

Blair watched Warwick's face carefully. 'I think they were pretty sure about you.'

'Based on what?' Warwick let those three words hang in the air. 'Because of my uniform? Because I wanted us to stay together? Because I wanted to perform a proper investigation of that docked ship? What kind of officer wouldn't insist on that!?'

Warwick pulled himself gently forwards, catching a handhold close to Blair.

'You're saying I must be the intruder because all the evidence points to me being exactly who I said I was?' He leaned in close. 'If you hadn't stopped me from doing my job, those people might still be alive.'

'It was that electrician who stopped you,' said Blair, firmly. 'Not me.'

'It's you now.'

Warwick returned to Lambert, leaving Blair alone at the base of the ladder. There was an uncomfortable silence.

'Alright.' Blair pushed himself towards the end of the corridor. 'We go over to life support, and we fix this thing together, just like we planned. Everybody keeps an eye on everybody else.'

Stirred by the blast of air rushing towards the hull, the corridors were even eerier than before. The beam of the torch picked out every drifting mote of dust, constellations shifting gently in the light. With the air now biting cold, the ship was like a tomb. Blair realised gradually that his mask was beginning to clog. He took it off and found that a plug of ice had formed inside the valve. He gave it a sharp tap against the wall, secured it to his face once more, and pressed on.

The life support backup was in an end room, just beside a tightly sealed pressure door. Blair shuddered. If they had all become trapped in the section beyond, there would have been no way of stopping the neighbouring cryonic bays from leaching all the heat from the air.

There was a rapid series of knocks from the pressure door, the metal straining to adapt to the irregular conditions. Blair began to prepare the generator that would power the backup system, but was hampered by the gun in his hand. He looked to his two companions.

'Lambert.' He held the magnetic anchor out, careful not to point it at him. 'Watch Warwick.'

Lambert nodded. 'Right.'

As the gun changed hands, Blair felt immediately vulnerable. Returning his attention to the generator, the feeling became more intense. After what had happened near the airlock, he couldn't turn his back on Warwick without someone looking out for him. However, there was no guarantee that Lambert was any more trustworthy. His only insurance was that, should one try to harm him, the other would retaliate.

Not knowing what effect the ship's centrifuge might have on navigation, Blair made sure the artificial gravity system was switched off. Then, he opened the valve on the generator's fuel tank and cranked the handle.

The machine juddered wildly for a moment before settling down, the noise shifting to a steady whine. Dim emergency lights snapped on one by one along the hall. More importantly, the control panel for the life support system flickered into life. He flipped the switch for the heaters and set atmosphere control to automatic. The small screen flashed through a flurry of warnings about contaminants, pressure, smoke particles, oxygen levels. Blair dismissed them. There was a rattle in the pipes along the corridor as the system began to replace the gas that had been lost when the airlock blew.

Blair could feel his ears popping. 'Once the pressure's back to normal, we should be able to force this door open.'

They waited.

'So...' Lambert broke the silence, but seemed unsure of his own voice. 'How come you fellows signed up to travel on the *Owen*?'

'What's it to you?' asked Warwick, more suspicious than belligerent.

Lambert gave a nervous chuckle. 'Just making conversation. We're in this mess together: seems as though we ought to know at least a little about each other.' He looked from Warwick to Blair, then back again. 'I got my start managing the L5 ore processing platform. The money's good, but what's it really good for? With all those ships heading in and out, you feel like everybody's going somewhere but you.'

Blair laughed. 'I was on a few of those ships myself. Got tired of always being shuttled from place to place. I saw the *Owen* as a chance to settle down more than anything: it's a one-way trip.'

'Seems as though it would be easier to settle down on Earth.'

'Not when you've been working with ships and satellites your entire career. Plus I'm not keen on open spaces. And the news... the news is never good.'

For a moment, the only sound was the steady hiss of nitrogen and oxygen flooding the section. Then Warwick spoke.

'It was the food riots.' His voice was quiet. 'I was assigned to a depot that had seen some trouble. There were arson attacks, bomb threats. The first day I was there, I saw a chap slip through a side gate. He had this big coat on, hood right down over his eyes, and he was carrying a bag. I shouted again and again for him to stop, but he didn't. He just carried on like it was the most natural thing in the world. So I shot him.'

Blair and Lambert waited for him to continue.

'He was a courier,' said Warwick at last. 'And he was deaf.'

'It could have happened to anyone,' said Lambert, consolingly.

'That's what the court decided. He should have gone through the checkpoint at the front. Someone should have cleared him.' Warwick shrugged. 'I did the only thing I could under the circumstances. But I still have to live with it.'

The three of them were silent once more.

Eventually, the pressure door shifted slightly, the locking mechanism disengaged. Blair moved towards it, then started back in surprise as the door opened of its own accord. McConnell burst out, clawing at the fabric of Blair's jumpsuit as he tried to climb past. Blair kicked him in the stomach, sending him spinning into the middle of the corridor where he flailed madly in midair, tears pooling on his face.

'Watch him!' Blair shouted to Lambert. 'Get the gun on him!'

'Calm down.' Warwick made no move, but spoke firmly. 'Just calm down.'

McConnell continued to drift, eventually managing to grab hold of a handrail. He stayed put, frantically gulping down air.

Blair took off his oxygen mask. 'What is it?' he asked. 'What's going on?'

'Close that door.' McConnell's attention was fixed on the narrow gap between the edge of the pressure door and the wall of the hallway. 'Close it!'

Not wanting to aggravate him further, Blair pulled the door shut.

All eyes were on McConnell as he stared wildly about the group.

'She's dead,' he said at last. 'Eva Roberts is dead.'

Five

Blair stared at Warwick. He had held this man at gunpoint – almost allowed him to asphyxiate – and yet here was absolute proof that he was not the murderer.

'I'm sorry,' he said. He couldn't manage anything more.

If Warwick heard the apology, he didn't acknowledge it. His mind was on the situation at hand. 'It's Clements,' he said, simply. 'It's Clements, or it's him.'

Lambert approached McConnell. 'Where's Clements?' he demanded.

McConnell's face was red. A string of mucus quivered between his nostril and his moustache.

'Where is Clements?' repeated Lambert.

McConnell took a ragged breath. 'I don't know.'

'Does she have the radio?'

Blair slid the pressure door open once more. Warwick passed him their group's radio.

Blair accepted it and pressed the transmitter. 'Clements!'

No response.

'Clements, where are you?'

He waited. He was just about to try again when her voice crackled through from the other end.

'It's McConnell!' she hissed. 'You have to help me! You have to stop him!'

Warwick took the radio mouthpiece. 'McConnell is here. Where are you?'

'I won't tell you. I'm not coming out. Not while he's…' she trailed off, but kept the transmit button pressed down. Blair could hear her rapid breathing in the background.

'We have to get the crew back together,' said Warwick. 'We have to sort this out. Right now it's just his word against yours.'

'It isn't,' said McConnell, quietly. He seemed to have calmed a little. 'Not necessarily.'

The group looked at him.

'Did any of you get a look at the docked ship? Was it...' he glanced around their faces, 'was it man-made?'

Warwick let go of the radio. 'What else would it be?'

'What if that ship didn't follow us from Earth? What if it came from our destination?'

Warwick turned away. 'This is insane.'

'I never told you my position on this ship.' McConnell fixed his attention on Lambert. 'That information isn't supposed to be common knowledge, and I didn't think it was relevant at the time. Before, I couldn't work out why Owen would have defrosted me. Now, having found that ship docked, I think I have an idea.'

'What is it you do?' asked Blair.

'I'm an exobiologist. I study life – what we expect life might be – on other planets.'

'There is nothing alive out there!' Warwick cut in.

Lambert put up a hand. 'Let him speak.'

'I wasn't originally part of this project,' continued McConnell. 'I was only brought in after long range spectroscopy revealed unusually high quantities of complex organic compounds on the planet's surface.'

'You're saying there's something alive out there?' put in Blair.

'That's far from certain, but it's more likely than not.'

'Do you really expect us to believe that something from another planet flew out to meet us, boarded, and is now trying to kill us?' Warwick was incredulous. 'That it, what, disguised itself as one of the crew?'

'I'm saying that it might not be anything to do with the crew!' McConnell turned to Lambert. 'You said that in an emergency, ten crew members would be defrosted. We know there's an extra person on board, but who's to say that extra person is the murderer?' He paused. 'I'm starting to wonder if that extra person is me.'

The group watched him carefully.

'Owen knew about the possibility of life on that planet. It knew about the possibility – however small – that we would come into contact with a non-human civilisation. Is it not at all possible that when it found the ship being boarded, it decided to defrost me in addition to the regular ten-person crisis team? Is it not at all possible that the intruder is someone beyond the eleven of us? That the computer chose eleven to deal with a twelfth?'

'It's possible,' answered Lambert, 'but it's not likely. The U.N. *Owen* is well equipped to avoid interstellar objects. If the sensors had picked up anything ahead of us, we would have had several weeks' warning. That ship almost certainly approached from behind. A small craft, no cargo? There's no doubt it could have caught up with us: the only question would be why.'

'We'll find out.' Warwick grabbed Blair by the arm. 'You're an engineer. You get the computer back online, and we'll have all the answers.'

Blair's stomach lurched. 'I... suppose so.'

The computer was the heart of the ship, as rugged as it was indispensible. Blair was fairly confident that getting it working would involve little more than flipping a reset switch. The problem was getting to it. He'd been trained to use a compression suit, but only in case of emergency. Had he known he would actually have to venture outside the ship, he would never have joined the crew.

Warwick picked up the radio mouthpiece once more. 'Clements? We need you back here. We've got a plan.'

The group waited. There was no answer.

'Fine.' Warwick let go of the transmit button and pulled himself over to the pressure door. 'We search room by room, hall by hall, and we find her. And we'll prove that there is nothing except us awake on board this ship.'

In the faint red light of emergency life support, the metal corridors were less imposing. With the heaters running, the cold was no longer a threat. The group moved methodically through the ship: Blair and Lambert in front, on the lookout for Clements; Warwick with the weapon behind, keeping McConnell in check.

For the first time since he had been thawed, Blair felt as though they were in control of the situation. Clements or McConnell, they had their murderer. He knew he could trust Lambert and Warwick, and more than that he knew they could trust him. All that remained was to restore the computer and identify the intruder.

Then they found the body, and his confidence vanished.

Eva Roberts remained fixed in place, one arm wedged between a handrail and the wall behind it. A cluster of small tools hovered beside her, shaken from the kit in her limp hand. Her head was tilted at an unsettling angle, the skin of her jaw drawn unnaturally taut. Disturbed by the air shifting as the group approached, her hair wafted aside and Blair caught sight of a long strip of plastic: someone had tightened a cable tie around her neck.

'What exactly happened here?' Warwick demanded.

'I don't know,' McConnell answered firmly. 'Clements was examining the navigation system. I was holding the light. When we started losing pressure, I… I panicked. I made a grab for a handhold and by accident I smashed the torch. The three of us got separated in the confusion. By the time I found Roberts…' he stared at the corpse clinging to the wall.

'Awfully easy to sneak up on someone in zero gravity.' Warwick put his face close to McConnell's. 'No footsteps. No need really even to move. You'd just drift right up to her and, why, you've got a ready-made noose right here.' He plucked another cable tie out of the air. 'Is that how you did it, then?'

'Please…' Fat beads of tears were forming on the bridge of McConnell's nose.

'Is that how you killed her!?'

McConnell sobbed quietly.

'He knows.' Warwick looked around at the others. 'He knows we'll be able to prove it was him. That's why he fed us that codswallop about aliens. So we'll be watching our backs and not watching him.'

Blair was certain McConnell's horror was genuine. Perhaps it was only horror at his own crimes, but then why hadn't he been as affected by the body in the computing hub? It didn't seem right. He put the question to Warwick: 'You don't think there's any chance it could have been Clements who did this?'

'I don't think there's any doubt it was him.' Warwick jabbed the improvised gun at McConnell. 'He couldn't tell us why he was here in the first place. Then, when it suits him, he makes up whatever story he likes. It's not a terribly convincing story, I'll admit, but at this point

I'm not sure what else he could have said. Three people went into this section alive before it was sealed off, and when we got it open there were just two. One of them killed our navigator, and I'll be damned if it was the young woman scared out of her wits in a corner somewhere.'

'So why did he do it?' The more Blair thought about it, the more the whole situation just didn't add up. 'Obviously this was going to attract suspicion. What reason could he have had to kill her when we'd know for certain that it was either him or Clements who did it?'

'Who knows?' Warwick cast a glance at McConnell, now hugging a handrail, his face turned to the wall. 'Maybe he's mad. Why else would anyone do something like this?' He paused. 'Or maybe she found something. Some kind of proof that he's the one who came in on that ship.'

'All the more reason to keep going,' said Lambert. 'One way or another, we'll have our answers.'

Blair looked at the tools surrounding Roberts' body, at the pearls of blood clinging to her jaw. 'She must have been trying to cut the tie,' he said. 'That's why she had her arm under the rail: so she could keep a hold on the wall and still use both hands.'

'It certainly looks that way.' Warwick didn't bother turning his head.

'So where's the knife?'

There were a sickening few seconds while everybody searched the air for it.

Warwick nodded at McConnell. 'Check him,' he said to Lambert.

McConnell broke out of his stupor, putting his hands up in front of him. 'Where would I hide something like that?'

Lambert ran his hands across the surface of McConnell's pocketless, insulated jumpsuit. 'Nothing.'

Blair hadn't expected there to be. 'Clements,' he said. 'We know she already found the body, otherwise how would she know that Roberts was dead?'

'They were both here at some time or another,' put in Lambert. 'McConnell told us as much, and Clements got the knife.'

'This changes nothing,' said Warwick, firmly. 'We keep

McConnell under control, and we find Clements. Then all we've got to do is keep an eye on both of them until we can get the computer running. We stick to that plan and everyone gets out of this just fine.'

'Even the intruder?' asked Lambert.

'Even the intruder.' Warwick was emphatic. 'There are four thousand people on board. When we get to our destination, there will be courts and judges. What happens then will be up to them.'

The group moved on more slowly than before, crawling hand over hand along the walls of the ship, checking any crevice where Clements could be hiding. Until they got the computer working, and they had all the facts, there would always be two suspects. Blair hoped that Warwick was right, that they already had the one they wanted, but still he was uneasy. Even if McConnell was the murderer, Clements was still unaccounted for, and she had armed herself.

'Stay where you are.'

Clements was waiting in the farthest corner of the section, tucked between a support strut and the hull itself. She held the utility knife at arm's length, as though the group at the end of the hallway had already drawn too close.

'Hold on.' Warwick put up a hand. 'Everything's under control. We just need to talk.'

Clements shrank back behind the strut. 'You can talk from there.'

'Alright. That's absolutely fine.'

'Life support's running again,' put in Blair. 'We've got some time.'

'That's right,' continued Warwick. 'We just need to get everything in order and then we can move on. We can get back to work. We just need to sort out what happened here first.'

'What happened here?' Clements pointed the knife at McConnell. 'He killed her! That's what happened. He smashed the torch and then, in the dark... so long in the dark.' She took a deep, ragged breath. 'I knew it was one of them. I knew I was shut in here with them, but I didn't find her until the lights came on.'

McConnell spoke softly. 'That's no different to what happened to me.'

'He's lying!' A fleck of spit escaped Clements' mouth and began to drift down the corridor. 'You've got to trust me, he's lying!'

'I do trust you.' Warwick held up a cable tie for her to see, then handed it to Blair. 'Hands behind his back.' He nodded at McConnell.

Blair took the tie, passed one end through the other, then pulled the loop closed over McConnell's wrists. The man didn't resist.

'Thank you.' Tears clung to Clements' eyes. She wiped them away with the back of her hand. 'Thank you, I—'

'Don't thank me just yet.' Warwick grimaced. 'We've got to watch both of you.'

'What do you mean?' Clements stared about the group. 'No! It was him! I know it was him! I've been in here alone with him all this time!'

'Exactly.' Warwick waited. 'It is my duty to maintain order and ensure the safety of everyone on board. I trust you, but until I know exactly what happened here – until I have all the facts – both you and McConnell are suspects.'

'But I know it was him! I know I didn't do it!'

'Then you know you can trust us. It's only until we can get the computer online and find out for sure.'

'She's stalling.' It was McConnell who spoke. 'She can't let you check the crew records.'

Warwick gave a mirthless laugh. 'A few minutes ago you thought we had an alien on board.'

'A few minutes ago I raised the possibility. But we've been through this section now, and we've found no evidence of that. You want the facts? I've cooperated – my hands are tied – but she's stalling.'

Clements gasped. 'You little—'

'Mark my words. When we get hold of the crew roster, she won't be on it. She's the one who came in on that ship.'

Clements hurled the knife at the floor. It struck the textured metal with a clang, then began to drift slowly back into the middle of the corridor, away from her. Lambert hesitated, looked at Clements, then made his way over to grab it.

'Only until we get the computer online.' Clements pulled herself out of the corner, her eyes fixed on McConnell's. 'And then we'll all know what's really going on here.'

She turned around and held her hands out behind her back.

Blair approached and gently drew a cable tie closed over her wrists.

He let out a breath he hadn't realised he'd been holding. It was over. McConnell or Clements, the murderer was under control.

'Navigation,' said Lambert.

'Right.'

Blair scrambled to get to the backup navigation system. Though he'd just put two of his fellow crewmembers – no, he reminded himself, only one – in restraints, he finally felt free. It was the first time he'd been able to move about the ship not only without fear, but without suspicion. Warwick and Lambert trusted him to get on with the job, and he trusted them to keep him safe.

Navigation was not as easy to start up as life support had been. Without a direct connection to the main computer, the ship's engines had to be controlled via radio. Still, the backup system was necessarily foolproof, and eventually he found himself just one button press away from putting the ship back on course.

'Brace!' he shouted.

He needn't have bothered. The ion thrusters kicked in with barely a shudder, and Blair himself felt only the slightest lurch, the change in velocity tugging him gently towards the back of the ship. He double-checked the figures on screen, and something wonderful dawned on him.

'We're accelerating!' he called to the others. 'We're not past the halfway point! We're still on course!'

Then his heart sank. They were safe. The ship was safe. But of the original crisis crew, fewer than half remained. Aldrin's group, Roberts, and that man in Hub Five had all given their lives trying to repair the ship. Roberts in particular had been determined to see the navigation system running as soon as possible, yet now it was apparent that the ship had been in no danger of overshooting its destination. If they'd only known that – if they'd known that they could spare the time – perhaps things would have turned out differently.

Lambert appeared at the end of the hall, Warwick and the others not far behind. 'Are you ready to make the crawl to the mainframe, or do you need a rest?'

Blair was exhausted. The threat of the steadily cooling ship, and the need for constant vigilance, had taken their toll. If there was ever an excuse to postpone his next ordeal, this was it.

'I'll do it now,' he answered. 'No sense keeping everybody waiting.'

Blair made his way to the remaining airlock and took a compression suit from the locker nearby. Lambert held onto Blair's feet while he pulled on the suit, then helped him connect the helmet and life support pack. If he noticed Blair's trembling hands, he said nothing.

There was a rush of air through the hollow seams of the suit, the pressure pulling the material tight. Struggling to remain calm, Blair found himself standing straight, arms by his sides, despite floating at a forty-five degree angle to the hallway floor. Facing the vacuum outside, the crushing discomfort was at least reassuring.

'The neck dam's not inflating.' Blair ran a thumb around the helmet's collar, resting snug beneath his jaw. 'I don't think I'm getting any air to the helmet at all.'

'Hang on.' Lambert tugged at the hose connecting helmet and pack.

There was a mechanical snap, and a blast of cold air ran across the back of Blair's head. Simultaneously, the neck dam filled to a much higher pressure, threatening to close his windpipe. He suddenly remembered Roberts, just metres away, the cable tie still locked around her throat. He pushed the image from his mind. Outside the ship, the collar would be the only thing keeping the air in his helmet.

'It looks as though you'll have to do this without anchors,' said Lambert. 'Warwick needs that modified one to keep the suspects under control. And the other…'

'Aldrin had it when the airlock blew.' Blair managed to force the words past the pressure of the neck dam. 'Sure it'll be fine. Handholds all the way. Not like there's anywhere to fall.' He cracked a nervous smile, forgetting that Lambert wouldn't be able to see it through the tinted visor.

'I'd count us lucky you managed to get the power back on. Aldrin's group had the generator as well.'

Blair's stomach lurched. He'd been so focused on getting the backup systems online, he hadn't thought ahead to the computer. Without power to the airlock, there was no getting to the mainframe, and without the mainframe, there was no going back to sleep. They'd come so close to being trapped in this one bay, and he'd never even realised.

Fighting the resistance of the compression suit, Blair pulled himself up the ladder into the airlock compartment. Inside were three large toggle switches beneath spring-loaded protective covers. He lifted the first cover and flipped the switch, sealing the door between himself and the ship's interior. The second switch started a bank of powerful vacuum pumps. Blair felt the neck dam gradually shift against his skin, the air in his helmet trying to push out past his collarbone. Inside the suit, his skin crawled and prickled as his flesh expanded to fill tiny cavities beneath the fabric. Besides his head, his body was entirely exposed to the vacuum: it was only the mechanical pressure of his suit that prevented his blood from boiling in his veins. A sweaty handprint on his visor steamed and turned to frost. He brushed away the brittle remnants with a gloved hand. When he was quite sure there was no air left in the chamber, he took a deep breath and flipped the final switch. The outer door slid open.

'All good?' asked Lambert, through the airlock radio.

'Seems to be.' Arms shaking, Blair began to heave himself out through the hatch into open space. 'I – !'

A staring face loomed at him from the edge of the airlock. The eyes were coated with a white film of ice, and a lattice of red frost covered the nose and mouth. As quickly as it had appeared, it was gone: a rigid form bouncing clumsily over the hatch.

'What is it?' Lambert's voice was urgent. 'What's going on?'

'It's one of Aldrin's team.' Blair watched the body drift away, a grim shadow against the blue haze of the ship's engines. 'I couldn't get... I didn't... they weren't recognisable.'

The body vanished into the blackness of space.

'Are you okay to continue?'

Blair looked back at the dim red space of the airlock. 'I have to be.'

Pulling himself over the edge of the airlock hatch, Blair crawled the short distance to the base of the spoke fixing this crew bay to the main body of the ship, a quarter of a kilometre overhead. He knew that if he looked up, he would see the other bays, all stretching out from the fuselage like spokes from a ship's wheel, but he kept his head down. He tried to imagine that there was a wall at his back, something to support him if he lost his grip on the ladder, but he knew there wasn't. The vacuum around him had a presence of its own.

Grasping the first rung of the ladder running along the spoke, Blair noticed a gentle force – ever so faint – tugging him away from the ladder and towards the poor frozen crewman receding into the distance. For a moment he couldn't work out what was causing this. Then, all at once, it became only too clear.

Blair had joked that there was nowhere to fall, but now it was apparent this wasn't the case. With the ship accelerating once more – albeit slowly – there was a slight sort of gravity, turning the space behind the ship into an endless drop. He would be, in effect, climbing along the underside of a ladder laid out flat. Those magnetic anchors would be sorely missed.

Blair clambered around to the other side of the spoke, considering that the same force of acceleration that pulled him away from one side would push him more firmly to the other. However, as he did so, he began to notice spots and flickers from the corner of his eye. Suddenly, sickeningly, he realised why. He ducked back behind the spoke.

Though the ship's ion engines could produce only a modest amount of thrust, decades of acceleration had brought the vessel up to a speed of thousands of kilometres per second. Travelling at perhaps thirty percent of the speed of light, the ship did not so much pass through the interstellar medium as obliterate it. The spots in Blair's vision were atoms of hydrogen and helium: ordinary matter converted into cosmic rays by the ship's astronomical speed. The only shelter from this bombardment of radiation – enough to kill him in mere minutes – was the spoke itself, but climbing in its shadow would mean clinging to the ladder against the acceleration of the ship. Blair took a deep breath and prepared to make the crawl to the mainframe, allowing himself just one last glance at the comparative safety of the airlock.

The dim hatch light was gone.

'Lambert?' he spoke through the radio. 'Is everything alright?'

No response.

'Lambert, can you hear me? Is the power still on?'

Nothing. Blair made a clumsy grab for the line of handholds leading to the airlock, and began to make the journey back.

'I can't do this without you. If that radio's not working, if...' but it wasn't the radio that was the problem.

Blair lifted the cover for the door control and flipped the switch. It sprang lifelessly back into its original position. He flipped it a few more times, desperately trying to trigger the mechanism.

'Lambert, you've got to fix this. I'm the engineer but I can't do anything from out here.'

There were twenty millimetres of steel between him and the crew. They'd never be able to pick up his voice on the portable radios. He slammed his fist against the door, deliberately at first, but then in a panic. Behind him, the hollowness of space seemed to seep in through the open hatch, the silence of the vacuum ringing in his ears.

The light flickered on.

As fast as he could, Blair reversed the procedure he'd used to leave the ship: closing the outer hatch, flooding the chamber with air, then opening the door to the crew bay. He flipped the last switch early, and was met with a violent blast of air rushing to fill the chamber. He dragged himself back inside the ship, and found Lambert waiting by the door.

'Thanks,' Blair gasped.

He suddenly noticed that Lambert was wearing a compression suit.

'What's with the suit?' he asked.

'Awfully hard to get by outside without one.'

Blair froze. It was not Lambert's voice.

It was Aldrin's.

Six

Blair glanced down the corridor, looking for any sign of the others. McConnell's alien idea had seemed so outlandish when he'd said it, but now it made a sort of sense: Clements and McConnell might not have been alone after all.

'What happened to you?' Blair asked.

'I got stranded outside.' The gold-tinted visor of Aldrin's helmet completely hid his face. 'I don't know how much longer I could have held out.'

Blair purged the air from the seams of his suit, releasing the pressure on his limbs. If there was going to be a confrontation, he'd need to be able to move freely. Aldrin, however, did nothing.

'You're not planning to go back out there, are you?' Blair nodded at Aldrin's still-pressurised suit.

'Goodness me, no.' Just then, Blair noticed that Aldrin was clutching one arm tightly to his side. 'I just don't think I should take the suit off right now.' Blood was seeping out from several layers of duct tape wrapped around his torso. 'Got caught in the blast.'

Blair wondered how long Aldrin had been inside the ship. If Roberts had been killed after they'd restored power, he could easily be responsible. However, his attention was diverted by something else entirely. 'Blast?'

'That docked ship was rigged with explosives. I don't know if we set them off or if they were on a timer and we just got unlucky, but either way our intruder didn't want anyone getting in there.'

'Do the others know you're here?'

'No. I headed for the life support console as soon as I got in – obviously someone must have started it up to get power to the airlock – but by the time I got there they were gone. I didn't like to call out in case it wasn't safe.'

'So you've been past life support.' If Aldrin had gone to that section of the ship, that would explain why they hadn't bumped into him already. However, it also would have given him ample time to come up with a story before approaching the rest of the crew. 'Any idea why the power went out just now?'

'I was trying to work that out when I heard you knocking. Fingers crossed it's just a mechanical problem. It happens when a ship stays frozen a long time. In any case, it's running again now.'

Of course. That was why Lambert hadn't been waiting for him: he was the only person free to go and fix it. 'I need to check on the others. It's probably best if I tell them you're here, rather than having them run into you unexpectedly.'

'Alright.' Aldrin remained clutching his side. He didn't look keen to go anywhere anyway. 'If you're sure.'

Blair pulled off his cumbersome helmet and worked his way back through the ship to the corridor where Warwick was watching the prisoners. However, when he got there, neither McConnell nor Clements were anywhere to be seen. Warwick was alone, resting with his back to one of the life support system's intake vents.

'Warwick?'

He didn't move. As Blair drew closer, he thought to look at the weaponised magnetic anchor. Sure enough, there was no screwdriver fixed behind the coil. Had he already taken his shot?

'Warwick, what's happened? Where's everybody else?'

But as Blair drew closer still, it was not the others that concerned him. Warwick was unconscious or worse, held in place not by his own power, but by the steady current of air being drawn into the vent behind him. Blair stretched out a hand to check Warwick's pulse, and found a bulb of plastic protruding from beneath his chin.

It was the handle of the screwdriver.

Five

'Is everything alright?' Aldrin had appeared at the end of the corridor.

With a sharp tug, Blair retrieved the screwdriver from Warwick's flesh. He set it back in place behind the anchor's magnetic coil and pointed the weapon at Aldrin. 'Don't come any closer!'

For a moment, both of them were silent, each watching the other.

'It was you,' said Aldrin. 'You killed the man in Hub Five. You set the explosives on that ship!' He was shouting, hoping that the others would hear.

'Don't waste our time, Aldrin!' Blair did the same. 'Everyone knows it couldn't have been me. You were in here when the power went out. You were in here after the pressure doors closed!'

Aldrin said nothing. Instead, he kicked off from the wall as hard as he could, flying at Blair with incredible speed. Acting instinctively, Blair thumbed the button on the magnetic anchor. The force generated by the coil dragged the screwdriver forwards violently, sending it whistling through the air. There was a sharp crack as it bounced off the top of Aldrin's helmet.

If Aldrin realised he'd been hit, he didn't show it. With no way of slowing down or changing course, he simply rammed right into Blair, head-butting him in the stomach with the full force of his lunge. Both hands still on the weapon, Blair crashed into Warwick and away from the wall.

Knowing that getting stuck in midair would leave him totally defenceless, Blair scrabbled for a handhold. He succeeded in grabbing the harness of Aldrin's suit. Using this purchase, Blair kneed his opponent in the ribs with all the force he could muster. Without gravity, he had no weight to put behind the blow, but the force of Blair's kneecap connecting with Aldrin's wound was all it took to turn things in his favour.

Doubled over in pain, Aldrin lost his grip on the wall. As the two careened into the centre of the corridor, Blair shifted his grip, locking an arm around Aldrin's throat, crushing the already-tight neck dam over his windpipe. Aldrin fought back, but with the seams of his suit still inflated he didn't have the range of movement necessary to force Blair away. The fight was over.

A broken cable tie drifted in front of Blair's face.

There was still every chance Aldrin was the murderer. Perhaps the cable tie was merely junk shaken into the air by the motion of the engines. Still, the possibility that one of the prisoners had taken Warwick by surprise, that Aldrin's reappearance was just unfortunately timed, made Blair loosen his grip.

'Lambert!' he shouted. 'Lambert get over here!'

A few terrible moments passed with Blair neither able to let go of Aldrin nor to keep an eye on his surroundings. If Clements or McConnell were the murderer, there was no telling where they were right now.

Finally, Lambert rounded the corner of the hallway. 'Clements has escaped,' he panted. 'I'm sorry, I—' he spotted Aldrin.

Blair explained: 'Aldrin was already in his suit when the airlock blew. He found his way back inside the ship after we got life support online. I don't...' Clements was loose, Warwick was dead, McConnell was who knew where. 'I don't know what to do.'

For a second, it looked as though Lambert didn't either. Then he spoke: 'Aldrin, if Blair lets you go can we count on you not to do anything stupid?'

'What?' croaked Aldrin. 'He attacked me!'

'That's not true!' snarled Blair. Then he thought back. He had set the screwdriver back into the modified anchor. If Aldrin had assumed that it had been Blair who killed Warwick, it was understandable that he would take that as an imminent threat.

Lambert moved closer. 'Aldrin's badly hurt. If he's innocent, we've got to help him. If he's not, we can handle him. But we won't get anywhere like this.'

'Alright.' Blair calmed himself. 'But remember there are two of us.' He released Aldrin.

Aldrin drifted, making no effort to catch hold of a handrail, both arms now clutched over his side. The sleeves of Blair's compression suit were streaked with fresh blood.

'We can't let this stop us,' said Lambert. 'Without the computer, none of the other passengers can be defrosted, and none of us can refreeze. One way or another, we have to deal with this so we can do what we need to do.'

'So what do we do?' asked Blair.

'Our top priority should be to get the computer running. There are four thousand people counting on us. But...' Lambert sighed. 'I don't think we can risk it. Not now.'

Blair could see his point. Before he'd headed out through that airlock, they'd had everything under control. Or they'd thought they had. If Warwick could be caught off guard while armed and ready, Lambert wouldn't stand a chance while overseeing Blair's crawl along the spoke. Trying to press on regardless would threaten not only the crisis crew, but everyone on board.

'We have to identify the intruder.' Lambert spoke firmly. 'The person responsible for these deaths knows that the crew records on the main computer will lead us straight to them. I have no doubt that they will do anything they can to prevent us from retrieving that information.' He stared at Blair. 'And with so few of us left, I don't know that we could stop them.'

'Why?' asked Aldrin. 'Why would anybody do this? What good does it do to escape justice if you doom yourself in the process?'

'Maybe they expect to repair the ship themselves,' offered Blair.

'I'm not sure there's even that much to it,' said Lambert. 'I'm not sure they ever planned this far ahead.'

'What?' Aldrin snorted. 'They got into a small craft – on their own – and boarded an interstellar colony ship without ever thinking through what they'd do once they were inside?'

Lambert shook his head. 'I think they must have had some idea of what they were doing to begin with. I think they must have intended to blend in with the crew somehow, but the man in Hub Five must have stumbled across them before they were ready. Perhaps they took the opportunity to get him out of the way, then couldn't cope. Perhaps everything since then is just covering it up.'

'Do you really think someone could commit four thousand murders to cover up one?' asked Blair, incredulous.

'Who would know?' Lambert spread his arms. 'With no one left, who would know?'

As a motive it seemed unlikely but, still, it was true: if the computer remained offline, the ship a dead hulk, no one would ever know what had become of them. Even if the journey was successful, even if they reached their destination and established a new world, they would have no contact with the Earth for at least a decade. They were utterly alone.

'I think we should turn on the centrifuge.' Blair looked down the corridor towards the life support backup. 'If I'm not going to be making the crawl for a while, we might as well. The gravity will make it harder for anyone to move around unnoticed.' He remembered what Warwick had said: it was awfully easy to sneak up on someone in zero gravity.

The centrifuge, like the engines, had to be controlled via radio. It should have been no more difficult to get it running, but Blair was distracted by the presence of Aldrin, and the knowledge that both Clements and McConnell were lurking somewhere on the ship. When the pressure doors had opened and they'd learned that Roberts had been killed, it had almost been a relief. Blair had known then that Warwick and Lambert could be trusted, and that Clements and McConnell could not. That had all changed the moment Aldrin reappeared.

'Why did the power cut out before?' asked Blair, realising that the life support system had likely had something to do with it. 'Was it a fault, or...'

Lambert answered: 'Someone fastened a clamp to the fuel line.'

Blair turned around, wanting to keep a close eye on Aldrin. 'While Warwick was watching the prisoners?'

Lambert shook his head. 'No. Or... maybe. It was fixed close to the tank. The generator probably would have run for a while just on what was left in the rest of the hose. I imagine whoever did it didn't want to be here when it cut out.' He stared at Aldrin. 'Or wanted it to look that way.'

Blair thought back. Aldrin could have sabotaged the generator any time after he got back inside. Clements could have slipped past and done it while they were preoccupied with Roberts' body. McConnell... 'Was McConnell ever alone in this section?'

'Not after the doors slammed shut. Maybe before.'

Blair ran through the process of starting the generator in his head. 'Before doesn't matter: I opened the fuel valve myself. If it had been clamped before then, we'd never have got it running.'

'Unless there was already fuel in the line.'

It didn't seem likely, but it was certainly a possibility: enough of a possibility that they couldn't discount McConnell as a suspect.

'Right,' said Blair. 'Everyone hold onto something and get your feet on the floor. I'm starting the centrifuge.'

He hit the button. A faint tremor ran through the ship as the vast motors in the main section shuddered into life. The crew bay, attached to main body of the ship by its quarter-kilometre spoke, began to revolve around it: slowly at first, but then faster and faster. All through the ship, there were clatters and bangs as unsecured objects began to shift about. Blair found himself being pressed gently against the wall by the force of the acceleration, then at the same time being dragged more firmly towards the floor – the outer edge of the ship – by centrifugal force.

As the motors finally came up to speed, Blair became able to stand and walk normally. The sensation was not entirely welcome. Accustomed to weightlessness, his knees trembled under his own weight, and his feet felt strangely heavier than his head: a side effect of the decidedly artificial gravity. He looked at Lambert, still braced against the wall, and Aldrin, sitting with his head between his knees. Blair had no doubt that both McConnell and Clements would be having similar difficulty adjusting to their new situation.

'We need to find the others,' said Blair.

'Give me a minute.' Aldrin released the air from his neck dam, then fumbled with the clasps connecting the helmet to the suit. With some difficulty, he pulled the whole thing off his head. His face was pale, his hair slick with sweat.

Lambert stared at him. 'If you can't—'

'I'm fine!' snapped Aldrin. He took a few shaking breaths. 'I'll be fine as soon as you can get the computer running. You can refreeze me and the medical team can deal with this whenever they're ready. I'll have all the time in the world.'

'We can't leave you unguarded,' said Lambert, firmly, 'and we can't just stay here. If you can't come with us…'

'One of us could stay with him,' offered Blair.

'So the other one can go hunting for a murderer on his own?' Lambert shook his head. 'We can't possibly take that kind of risk. The two of us can't afford to split up, and we can't afford to leave Aldrin unsupervised.'

Suddenly, Blair grasped what Lambert was suggesting. 'You mean… you think we should get rid of him?'

'That won't be necessary.' Grabbing hold of one of the handrails on the walls, Aldrin hauled himself to his feet. He swayed about unsteadily, held up partly by his pressurised suit, but remained standing nonetheless. 'Let's get moving.'

The slow, methodical march through the ship was quiet and unnerving. Blair took the lead, keeping the magnetic anchor pointed around each new corner, training it on each potential hiding place in turn.

'You said Clements had escaped – you saw her?'

'Her hands were free,' said Lambert. 'And there's something else.' He brought out the utility knife she'd given up. 'The blade on this is a couple of sections shorter than it should be. I think she snapped a bit off before we took it.'

'Enough to use as a weapon?'

'No, but enough to slice through a cable tie.'

'How about McConnell?'

'I don't know.'

That troubled Blair. If Clements had thought to conceal a piece of blade before she was restrained – before Blair and the others had even caught up with her – that was extremely suspicious. It also didn't bode well for McConnell. With his hands tied behind his back, he would have found it nearly impossible to move about in zero gravity, especially in the dark.

The group passed an empty suspension tank, its remaining fluid trickling out of the hatch and down the wall, and Blair realised that it was his own: they were walking down the same corridor he'd passed through when he first woke up. They were approaching Hub Five – the first room – and within it the first body.

Lambert tugged the door open, Blair keeping the anchor ready in case Clements or McConnell were waiting on the other side. However, there was no one inside but the dead man with the extinguisher, now lying face down in a drift of congealed blood.

'We've been through almost the entire ship.' Aldrin was exhausted, his voice shaking. 'What if they passed us? Skirted around through one of the other corridors?'

'Then we do another sweep.' Lambert began a lap of the computing hub, checking any space large enough to hide a person.

Blair's attention, however, was occupied by something else. 'Where's the axe?'

Lambert and Aldrin stared at the body in the corner.

'Could it have worked loose when we turned on the gravity?'

'It'd be on the floor.'

'Maybe it's under him.'

It was a definite possibility. As the centrifuge had begun to spin, it had pulled everything to the floor by the back wall. The axe could easily have ended up under the body, or the slush of blood and extinguisher foam piled alongside it.

Blair said what everyone was thinking: 'Someone should check.'

Nobody stepped forwards.

'We need to know.' Blair wasn't sure if he was trying to persuade the others or himself. 'We can't let something like that go unaccounted for. We need—'

'It's here.'

Blair whirled around, pointing the anchor at the other door. McConnell was there, the axe in his hands, a trickle of blood running from his forehead down to the end of his nose. Aldrin made a pitiful lurch away from him, clutching the handrails on the wall for support. McConnell didn't move.

'Drop it,' said Blair. 'I won't ask again.'

McConnell threw the axe down in front of him. It hit the metal floor with a clang that echoed through the ship.

'I only wanted it to cut the cable tie.' He held his hands up, showing the raw rings around his wrists. 'That's all, I assure you.'

'Where did all the blood come from?' asked Lambert.

'It's mine.' McConnell touched a hand to his scalp. 'I heard a struggle after the power went out. Pushed off the wall to get away and went headfirst into a handrail. Damn near knocked myself out.'

'Then where's Clements?'

McConnell's mouth fell open. 'She's still alive?'

Blair took a step closer to McConnell, brandishing the anchor. 'Why wouldn't she be?'

'I thought I heard a shot! I thought Warwick...' McConnell looked about the group. 'He's not with you.'

'If you thought Warwick shot Clements, why did you run?'

'I thought that was what happened. I didn't know for sure. Getting out of the way – waiting for a group – seemed like the safest thing to do.'

Blair couldn't argue with that. It was clear there had been a struggle. Assuming he was telling the truth, McConnell must have believed that it had been Clements who had attacked Warwick. That being the case, fleeing the area would have been quite reasonable. If Warwick had overpowered his assailant, the murderer would have been exposed and McConnell would no longer have been under suspicion. If Warwick had been overpowered, McConnell would almost certainly have become the next victim, had he remained where he was.

Blair struggled to piece together the events of the past hour. Both Clements and McConnell had escaped their restraints, and Aldrin's movements could not be known. There was so much that escaped him, so little that he knew for sure. And yet a few small facts had begun to slot together: Aldrin was badly injured, and it seemed unlikely that he could have bested Warwick, even with the advantage of surprise; McConnell had been under constant supervision since they had released the pressure doors, so would have had barely any opportunity to sabotage the generator; Clements had escaped their notice for some time, and had cut the cable tie around her wrists with a concealed blade. Blair had no proof, but he had his suspicions.

'I...'

Blair looked over to see Aldrin stagger into the middle of the room and fall against a console.

'I don't...' Aldrin collapsed to the floor.

Blair started towards him, then remembered McConnell. He kept the anchor trained on him. 'Lambert, help Aldrin.'

Lambert dashed over, but merely stood there, staring.

'Get a medical kit or something!' snapped Blair.

'And do what?' Lambert's hands hovered over the wound in Aldrin's side. A trickle of blood ran from between the layers of tape swaddling the injury. 'Do I move him? Do I take the suit off?'

'Just do something!'

'I don't know what I can do.'

Blair remembered his struggle with Aldrin. He remembered bringing his knee into Aldrin's ribs. 'Take the anchor.'

Forcing the device into Lambert's hands, Blair knelt down beside Aldrin but found he could do no more. Without any training, any medical supplies, the situation was hopeless. Still he couldn't bear to simply watch. He unbuckled Aldrin's life support pack and disengaged the magnetic clamps, leaving it tethered only by the air hose that kept the suit pressurised. Having freed him of the pack, Blair laid Aldrin out flat on his back and pressed as hard as he could on the wound, trying to stop the bleeding.

A few minutes passed. Blair kept his whole weight on the wound, determined to do what he could and yet knowing that it could never be enough. The damage had been done.

At last, Lambert spoke. 'We can't afford to stay here with him.'

Blair took a hand off Aldrin's chest and pressed two fingers beneath his jaw. If there was a pulse, it was too faint to feel. He was beyond help now.

'We don't have to.' Blair stood. 'He's gone.'

Four

Blair couldn't take his eyes off the body. When he'd found Warwick floating dead in the corridor, he'd been so sure that Aldrin was responsible. In that moment, he'd had no doubt. Now Aldrin had died of his wounds, and Blair was left with the knowledge that he may have had a hand in the death of an innocent man. It was still possible that Aldrin had been guilty. Even if he hadn't been, there was no guarantee he would have survived their ordeal. But Blair could take no comfort from that: the uncertainty weighed on his mind as much as the guilt.

'What's that?'

Blair looked at Lambert. Lambert nodded at Aldrin's detached life support pack, keeping the weapon trained on McConnell.

The magnetic clamps of the pack had picked up some tiny scraps of steel. Injured, dragging himself along the wall, Blair supposed that Aldrin could have dislodged all kinds of debris. However, there was one piece that was clearly the odd one out. It was larger than the others – an object formed of stamped and folded metal – though it had clearly once been a part of something else. It struck Blair as somehow familiar. He leaned over to pick it up.

'Wait!' Lambert lunged towards him.

Blair snapped back upright.

'Aldrin was on that other ship, right? Or at least near it.'

Blair thought back. He wasn't sure Aldrin had ever actually gone inside, but if he'd been in his suit at the time of the blast then he must have been close. 'Yeah.'

'That looks an awful lot like the release catch of a suspension tank.'

Blair stared at the bent strip of metal. Lambert was right: he remembered tugging at the very same catch to open the door when he first woke up. And of course it looked familiar: it had been the last thing he'd seen before he'd been frozen, and the first thing he'd seen when this nightmare had begun.

'That shuttle.' He looked to Lambert. 'Aldrin said—'

'It only had one tank. Whoever's on board with us,' said Lambert, his voice quivering, 'whoever's not supposed to be here, they've put their hand on that. They've put their hand on that, and I'll bet they weren't wearing gloves.'

Blair's heart leapt.

McConnell spoke up: 'Warwick's fingerprint idea. Only…'

'Only he's not here to do it any more.' Blair's heart sank once more.

'Who says it has to be Warwick that does it?' Lambert handed Blair the anchor once more and stooped to examine the catch, still fixed firmly to the pack's magnetic clamp. 'The point of using fingerprints was that we could do it without the computer, without electricity, without anything but a dusting of powder and a strip of tape. But the same things that make that practical without modern technology make it practical without specialist training.'

'Now hold on.' McConnell put up his hands. 'This is a life-or-death situation we're in. I don't know if any of us are qualified to make a decision on something like that – not with so much at stake! Maybe if Warwick himself could—'

'Do you think Warwick ever dusted a fingerprint before?' Lambert stood up. 'Do you think Warwick, a security officer on board an interstellar craft, ever went out with a jar of… of ground-up coal? And a little paintbrush? Do you think they trained him to do that, just in case he ended up in a situation where there was no surveillance footage, no DNA testing, no crew records?' He looked down at the release catch, the one flimsy connection between the murderer and their crimes. 'No. Warwick knew that fingerprinting wouldn't be ideal, but he also knew it was the best we could hope for. What he said then is what we'll do now.'

Blair had to agree. Of the nine people he'd first met in that narrow corridor, only three remained. They had lost so many. However, a faint doubt still gnawed at him. 'We need Clements,' he said. 'We need everybody's prints. Yours, mine, everybody's. Just to make absolutely certain there's no doubt.'

'None of us have touched that catch,' said Lambert, firmly. 'Not since it got trapped on Aldrin's pack.'

'I had him by the throat,' said Blair. 'I grabbed hold of the harness. I can't say for sure I never put a finger on the catch. And what if it was

Aldrin? What if it was him who boarded us?' He looked once more at the white face, the glassy eyes. 'We check everyone. All of us, and Aldrin, and then we'll know for sure.'

'Alright. But we check McConnell first.' Lambert started towards the corridor where the ten of them had first assembled. 'The store-room here should have everything we need.'

As Lambert began down the hallway, there was a crash from the storeroom. Blair rushed to the door and caught a glimpse of a jump-suit vanishing around the corner.

'Clements!' Lambert broke into a run.

Blair hesitated, torn between pursuing Clements and guarding McConnell.

McConnell took a step towards the door, eyes on the weapon in Blair's hand. 'I'm going after them. Alright?'

'Right! Go!'

As Blair ran after McConnell, the sounds of a struggle began to echo down the hall. There was a sharp clang as something hard struck a surface, then the rapid click of a utility knife being extended.

Blair rounded the corner. 'Don't move!'

Lambert and Clements were on the floor, one struggling to hold on, the other to get away. At the sound of Blair's voice, they both froze. Clements was clutching a small section of steel blade, Lambert the knife it had been snapped from. A long cut ran from the back of his hand to halfway down his forearm, the sleeve of his jumpsuit hanging open like an unbuttoned cuff. Cautiously he shifted to one side, giving Blair a clear shot at Clements.

'Drop it.' Blair nodded at the sliver of blade.

Clements let go, but the slim bit of metal remained stuck to her fin-ger: in the struggle, it had bitten into her skin. She tugged it out and threw it away. 'I only wanted to be left alone. To stay out of the way.'

'What are you waiting for?' cried McConnell. 'Shoot her!'

Clements had been in the best position to sabotage the generator. Clements had been with Roberts when she had been killed. Clements had hidden a blade before she was found and cut her bonds after the power went out. And now, Clements had attacked Lambert rather than rejoin the group. Clements had been present for every tragedy to befall the crew, and here was an opportunity to make sure that there would be no more tragedies at all.

Blair gestured at her with the anchor. 'Get up.'

'You can't be serious!' McConnell took a step forwards.

'Quiet!' Blair shot a glance at him. 'Somebody in this room is a murderer, and we've got a good chance of finding out who it is once and for all. I'll be damned if I'm going to see anyone else die before we do that.'

'But it was her! We know it was her!'

'A little while ago we "knew" it was you.'

McConnell immediately went quiet.

'Clements gets the same chance as anybody else.' Blair looked at Lambert. 'Get the things to take her prints.'

Lambert looked up from his lacerated arm, blinked, then burst out laughing.

Blair stared at him, afraid he'd lost his mind.

'Sorry.' Lambert struggled to control himself. 'It's just... I said, didn't I? I said everything we needed was in that storeroom, and wouldn't you know it, Clements was too!'

The group assembled in Computing Hub Five, gathered around Aldrin's body. Lambert brought out a roll of white electrical tape and a tub of dark grey powder flux.

'Alright.' He stooped over the release catch stuck to Aldrin's life support pack. 'Let's see if we have anything to work with.'

With painstaking care, Lambert shook a fine coating of flux over the surface of the metal. Then, touching it only by the very edges, he tapped the catch against the floor, getting rid of the excess.

'We've got prints.'

McConnell breathed a sigh of relief. Clements remained silent. Blair watched her, weapon still in hand. He was determined to have all the facts – Aldrin's death weighed heavily on his mind – but still he found himself waiting to hear that the prints were hers.

Lambert rubbed the powder flux over his hands, then pressed his fingertips to a strip of tape. He cut that section from the roll and marked it with an 'L.'

'Seems neat enough.' Slowly, he approached Clements, making sure not to put himself between her and Blair. 'You next.'

With no particular care, Clements dunked a hand in the tub of powder and slapped it on the tape.

Lambert scowled. 'We can do this as many times as we need to.' He stepped over to McConnell. 'Now you.

McConnell dutifully provided his fingerprints.

Lambert turned to Blair. 'You were quite insistent that we check yours too.'

'We check everyone's,' said Blair. 'We make absolutely sure.'

'Alright then.' Lambert held out his hand for the magnetic anchor. Blair exchanged it for the flux and tape.

Though he would be in no danger even if the fingerprints on the catch were his own, Blair found his hand trembling as he pressed it to the tape. Marking the strip with a 'B,' he stood.

'Now then…' Anchor still in hand, Lambert stepped over to the metal catch and the strips of tape. 'Let's see who the culprit is.'

Blair stared at the sets of prints. Three were neat, the ridges of the fingers standing out clearly. One – marked with a 'C' – was barely distinguishable, a smear of blood marring the impression of Clements' index finger entirely.

'Hang on.' Blair caught Lambert by the shoulder. 'We haven't taken Aldrin's yet.'

Lambert stared at him.

Blair reached for the anchor. 'We need his. We still can't rule out the possibility that he was behind all this.'

'Quite right.' Lambert passed the anchor back, then set to work with the powder and tape.

Blair kept his attention fixed on Clements. He didn't want to see Lambert manoeuvring Aldrin's dead fingers. When his prints had been taken, his tape too was smeared with blood: it was now collecting beneath his body in a small pool.

'What do you make of them?'

Lambert compared the prints on the tapes to the smears on the release catch. He spent a long time examining each and every one.

Finally, he spoke: 'It's Clements.'

Blair had expected noise and activity. He had expected Clements to run, as she had done when Lambert had approached the storeroom, or to strike out, as she must have done when the man with the extinguisher blundered into this very room. Instead, there was silence. They'd had their trial, but who would carry out the sentence? The anchor, the screwdriver poised behind the coil, was heavy in Blair's hand, but nobody stepped forward to take it from him.

It was Clements herself who broke the silence. 'Alright. It was me.' She spoke so quietly that, had the room not been completely silent, no one would have heard her. 'Back on Earth, I did something that I... well...' she gave a weary smile. 'Why should I tell you? I snuck on board the *Owen* for a new life, a new chance. I set the explosives to destroy the evidence. But I never knew they'd breach the hull, and it wasn't me who put the axe through those cables.' She looked up, her gaze meeting Blair's. 'I never killed anyone. I... never meant to kill anyone.' She turned to face McConnell. 'I'm no murderer.'

'What?' McConnell stared at her. 'What are you implying?'

'Roberts.' She shook her head. 'All I wanted was to blend in, so why would I kill one of the crew when there were just three of us in the section? Why draw attention to myself like that?'

'And why would I have any more reason?' asked McConnell. He stepped over to the axe and picked it up, the head scraping ominously across the floor.

'I was told there would be someone on board to help me cover my tracks. I think you knew I wasn't one of the crew. I think you knew that when this finally came out, everyone else would be on your side.'

'They nearly killed me!' McConnell pointed the axe at Blair and Lambert. 'When I told them Roberts had been murdered, they thought I did it!'

Blair stepped to one side, trying to keep Clements in his sights. 'McConnell, get out of the—'

'But they held off this long, didn't they!?' Clements screamed. 'They held off long enough for you to pin all this on me!'

McConnell made a wild swing with the axe. Clements jumped back, hitting the wall with a thud. Blair started forwards, trying to get a clear shot but knowing he couldn't risk it. McConnell swung again, and Clements made an ungainly dive, the axe head catching her shoulder before putting a dent in the wall. She fell across the corpse at the back of the room. As McConnell hefted the axe once more, she brought something up from the drift of blood and foam: it was the extinguisher.

Driving the heavy cylinder forwards with all her might, Clements caught McConnell full in the face. He reeled backwards, and Clements used the space to bring her makeshift weapon down hard on the top of his head. McConnell fell, and Clements ran.

'Stop!' shouted Blair, as she made a dash for the corridor. 'Stop or I'll—' She was at the door. He took the shot.

There was a sickening thud as the screwdriver punched into Clements' back, then another as she hit the floor and skidded. She was out of sight, but he could still hear her struggling to stand up, to breathe. Lambert picked up the axe and walked swiftly out of the room. There was a bang, and the struggle ceased.

Lambert returned, looking very pale.

'What if she was telling the truth?' asked Blair, after a pause. 'What if McConnell really…'

Lambert looked at McConnell, lying face down on the floor. He was motionless, a clear fluid leaking from his nose. 'I don't know,' said Lambert, exhausted. 'I don't think it matters any more.'

Two

Blair and Lambert worked in silence, reconnecting the severed cables. There was no telling what kind of damage had been done to the computing hub, but Blair was confident that the mainframe in the central section of the ship would merely need to be reset. Perhaps Clements had been counting on that. Perhaps she hadn't thought that far ahead.

'Done.' Blair extinguished the welding torch. 'Owen should be able to diagnose any problems with the equipment in here, so the next step is to head out to the mainframe.' He remained staring at the patched-up cables, and their rough covering of heat-shrink tubing. He tried to avoid looking at the scene behind him, the bodies still lying where they had fallen. This time around, venturing outside the ship almost seemed preferable to remaining inside.

'Right.' Lambert too seemed utterly absorbed by their work on the cables. 'No time like the present.'

They walked to life support and shut down the centrifuge, so that Blair would not have to fight gravity on his way to the centre of the ship. Then, weightless once more, they made their way back to the airlock. Blair forced his head into the helmet and repressurised his suit, Lambert double-checking the connections.

Blair worked the airlock in a stupor. After the events of the last few hours, the danger of decompression, of stepping outside the mechanically maintained world of the ship, hardly fazed him. Even the crawl to the main section, with the infinite expanse of space yawning apparently below him, passed by in a daze. Now that he had Aldrin's still-functioning magnetic anchor, there was little chance of becoming separated from the ship. It was over. Just this one final task, and he was done.

There were no buttons at the other end of the ladder. No lights or switches. Blair closed a gloved hand over the simple release wheel of the hatch. He felt the metal squeal as he turned it, but he heard no sound. There was only his own breathing, and the regular snap of the air regulator.

'I'm in,' he said over the helmet's radio.

'Good luck,' replied Lambert, from the console by the airlock door.

Blair pulled himself through the hatch, then tugged it closed. Immediately inside was the machinery to turn the centrifuge: the motors that lent the bays at the end of each spoke the illusion of gravity. Further along the ship's vast fuselage was the mainframe that controlled all the equipment on board. Blair pulled himself over to it. The small monitor, the status lights, the racks and racks of circuit boards were all dead. The machine responsible for the lives of all the frozen passengers was itself utterly helpless.

Blair opened an electrical cabinet and reset a line of breakers. A small button at the end of the line came to life, illuminated by a single blinking LED. Blair pressed it.

Immediately, the ship shuddered into action. Lights flickered. Coolant pumps began to rumble. The small screen bolted to the racks of circuit boards flashed through several pages of dense text, then refreshed, displaying only a single word: 'Initialising…'

It was replaced a moment later by: 'Ready.'

Blair spoke into his helmet's microphone: 'Owen?'

'Awaiting instructions.' The computer's synthetic voice crackled through the speakers in his helmet. 'There has been an incident. Electrical systems require reset on spokes: one, four, five. May I continue?'

'Yes.' Blair felt a wave of relief wash over him.

'Systems reset successfully. The terminal on spoke five has suffered a critical malfunction. Redundant components are available. May I continue?'

'Yes.'

'Spoke five terminal operational. Catastrophic loss of pressure detected at five primary airlock. Suspected hull breach. Recommend Aldrin, Brett, to perform repairs. Blair, Moreau, to supervise.'

'Aldrin is dead.' Blair didn't recognise the other names, but remembered the man with the extinguisher, and the three crew who'd been killed when the airlock blew. 'Brett and Moreau too. We've lost everyone except me and Lambert. There aren't enough of us left to repair that breach.'

'This is a serious incident. It will be recorded and reported to the board of directors upon arrival. Please describe, providing as much detail as possible—'

'Owen, stop.' Blair was glad to be able to hand responsibility to the computer, but just now there was one more thing he had to do. 'I need to know who you selected for the crisis team. I need to know now.'

Owen began to rattle off names. 'The team selected was as follows: Edmund Aldrin, engineer; Wilson Blair, engineer; Ellie Brett, engineer; Felix Lambert, logistics manager and designated emergency response overseer; James McConnell, role withheld; Andrew Marlowe, safety inspector; Ian Moreau, engineer; Eva Roberts, navigation officer; Toby Roberts, electrical technician; Lawson Warwick, security officer.'

That was it. All ten crew members accounted for, and no mention of Clements. Still, one small detail nagged at him. 'Why was Lambert chosen to lead the team?'

'Felix Lambert was nominated by the board of directors to ensure continuity of command.'

'So you didn't select him?'

'I did not.'

'He was chosen beforehand? Before the launch?'

'That is correct.'

'He knew he would be defrosted in an emergency?'

'Felix Lambert was made aware of his responsibilities well in advance. He would not have been given the position if he were not prepared to accept it.'

There was a pause.

Owen spoke again: 'Are you prepared to give your report now?'

'No.' Blair made his way back towards the hatch, towards the ladder. 'Not just now.'

The spoke was so long that Blair's light could not pick out his destination. Soon the fuselage too vanished into the darkness. Beyond the short stretch of the ladder illuminated by his suit, the ship was nothing more than a shadow against the stars.

Lambert's voice came through over the radio. 'Everything alright? The lights came on a while ago. You've been gone a long time.'

'Just making sure everything's up and running.' Blair tried to sound casual. 'I don't want to have to come out here a third time.'

'Where are you now?'

Blair had no idea. He hadn't thought to count the rungs. 'Nearly there.'

It turned out that it was true. In the distance, the faint orange light of the airlock came into view.

'I checked with Owen,' said Blair, offhandedly. 'About Clements. She was definitely the one who came on board, but there's no telling whether or not she was telling the truth about the murders.'

'Probably best not to think about it.'

Blair crawled closer to the light, closer to the airlock. 'Probably. It's just… you have to wonder why she'd lie. She seemed to know it wouldn't save her.'

'She was goading McConnell. And it worked. Even if she was telling the truth, even if he was the murderer, what does it matter? He's dead too. It's over.'

Blair was nearly at the end of the spoke. 'I wonder, though. I wonder if Clements was telling the truth about the murders, but wrong about McConnell.'

'Everybody who was behind those doors when Roberts was killed – everybody – is dead.' Lambert was firm. 'Whoever it was, it's over now.'

'Awfully easy to sneak up on someone in zero gravity. Just like Warwick said.' Blair reached the end of the ladder. 'But what if nobody tried to sneak up on Roberts? What if she was trying to sneak up on someone else?'

Lambert was silent.

'You weren't with me and Warwick when Aldrin's friend pulled that anchor on us. You were waiting just outside. Quite the commotion, wasn't it? I wouldn't have been surprised if someone else had come to intervene: especially someone who'd been suspicious of Warwick from the beginning. Wouldn't it make sense for Roberts to break away from her group, if she thought the murderer had already been discovered?'

'She was killed on the other side of those pressure doors!'

'No. She may have died on the other side of those pressure doors, but I'll bet she was right behind me on the ladder when you slipped the noose over her head.'

'If what you're saying is true, don't you think it would be unwise to tell me all this?'

'If what I'm saying is true, I don't think it'll make a difference.'

Blair reached the airlock. The outer door was closed, a red hot patch of metal glowing dimly in the centre. The flame of a cutting torch – no doubt wedged against the other side of the door – peeked through a small hole in the steel.

'Owen,' Blair's voice trembled. 'Open the airlock.'

'The outer door has been perforated,' responded the computer, as calmly as it would have told him the time. 'I can't do that without venting the section's atmosphere.'

'Owen, do it anyway.'

'I can't do that. The outer door has been perforated.'

'Owen, open the airlock now!'

The ship made a sudden lurch, and the magnetic anchor tethered to Blair's wrist skittered across its surface, forcing him to snatch at a handhold. His toes slid across the metal as the hull began to move. It took him a moment to realise what was happening.

'Owen, turn off the centrifuge! I'm still outside! Turn off the centrifuge!'

'Owen,' Lambert's voice came over the radio, 'disregard Blair's instructions. He's gone mad. He cannot be allowed on board.'

Blair put an arm through a ladder rung and clasped his free hand around that wrist. Inside, he'd been pressed against the wall as the centrifuge began to spin. Here, there was no wall. There was only the infinite expanse of space, the stars whipping past on the endless horizon.

'Owen!' Blair struggled to keep his helmet pressed to the hull, to prevent its weight pulling him head over heels into space. 'It's Lambert who's mad. Open the airlock. It's the only way to stop him now.'

'You are at an impasse.' Owen's voice was almost drowned out by Blair's visor rattling against the hull. 'I am not qualified to act as an arbitrator in such a situation. A record will be made. The board of directors will be notified.'

The centrifuge gradually came up to speed, and Blair found himself being pressed safely against the hull. Still he did not relax his grip. The airlock was useless. There was nowhere to go.

Blair remembered Aldrin. How long had he waited out here before the power came on? Had he spent that time clinging to this same handhold, hoping that someone would come to the airlock, or had he only made the crawl over once the lights came on in his depressurised section of the ship?

Lambert's voice crackled into the helmet once more. 'Still there?'

Blair shut off the radio. Arms trembling from the effort of holding on, he began to make his way along the hull, towards the blown-out airlock that Aldrin must have passed through. Cosmic rays danced across his retinas, but he pressed on. There was no other way. Finally, he came to the airlock: a ring of scarred, twisted metal punched into the surface of the ship. Careful to avoid puncturing the seams of his suit on any sharp edges, Blair dropped inside.

The floor of the lost section was littered with fragments of metal, scattered by the blast. The inner door of the airlock had been blown against the opposite wall, crushing several pipes. The body of one of Aldrin's team lay nearby, frozen to the floor. Blair picked his way through to the pressure door, the electrician still pinned exactly where he had been when it closed on his arm. Blair tried not to look, instead examining the door itself. Owen had refused to open the airlock Lambert had sabotaged, but this pressure door was entirely mechanical, neither dependent on nor connected to the ship's electronics. The computer had no control over it.

Picking up a welding torch from the toolkit Aldrin had taken, Blair got to work. Heaving the airlock door back into position, he set about fixing it in place. Mangled by the blast, it no longer formed anything like a seal against the void, but it was the only piece of material in the section large enough to do the job. The door welded, Blair tugged a sheet of foam insulation from a fissure in the wall. This he spread across the airlock door, plastering it down with pipe sealant.

The result was a thin, airtight barrier: not a full repair, but hopefully enough to do the job.

Several fluorescent oxygen generators had emerged from the walls here, just as they had done in Blair's section when the pressure dropped. Gathering every one he could find, Blair made a pile and activated them all. With no air, no atmosphere to wick away the heat, the generators burned ferociously hot. Taking a wrench to one of the pipes, Blair began to drain the liquid nitrogen from a neighbouring cryonic bay. A small trickle dropped from the hose port, hit the searing oxygen generators, and boiled on contact. He opened the valve further, ducking away from the spitting nitrogen.

As Blair hurried back towards the pressure door, he checked the makeshift seal over the airlock, already bulging outwards under the force of the gas filling the section. As he reached the pressure door, he heard the hull creaking: there was now enough of an atmosphere to carry sound. Despite this, however, the door to the rest of the ship remained locked shut. Blair tugged at it with all his strength, knowing that every second he took was another second for the airlock to fail under the pressure.

There was a squeal from the hastily welded airlock. Blair grabbed a large screwdriver and jammed it into the place where the electrician's crushed arm was caught in the pressure door's seal. He pulled against it, levering the door open far enough for a blast of air to rush through from inside the ship. The pressure equalised, and the mechanism holding the door closed disengaged. Blair shoved it open and stepped through. An instant later, there was a screech of metal on metal. The airlock gave way, and the pressure door clamped shut once more.

An electric snap rang through the ship. Something whistled through the air, thudding into Blair's shoulder. Feeling more surprise than pain, he tried to see what had happened, but the neck dam of his helmet wouldn't allow it. Instead, he looked along the corridor. Lambert was there, slotting another screwdriver into the weaponised magnetic anchor.

Blair staggered towards the ladder, expecting any minute for Lambert to shoot him in the back, as he himself had shot Clements. There was another snap, and Blair stumbled in surprise, but the missile never found its mark. There was a resounding clang as the screwdriver ricocheted off the wall ahead of him. Spurred on by the knowledge that Lambert had spent his shot, Blair tumbled down the hatch, jarring the screwdriver in his flesh and almost landing on Clements, face down in the hallway below.

Something dug into Blair's back, and he realised that he was lying on the axe. He picked it up with his good hand, ready to strike at Lambert as he came down the ladder: the only place where the axe held an advantage over the gun. But though Lambert's shadow passed over the mouth of the hatch, he did not descend.

'Why are you doing this?' shouted Blair, the helmet making his own voice ring in his ears.

'This was simply the easiest way.'

Blair shrank back against the wall, wary of Lambert taking a pot shot through the hatch.

'McConnell was telling the truth, not that he knew all of it. There is life where we're going. There's no doubt about it. And that's why we can't be allowed to get there. Mankind has all but destroyed one world. I won't see us destroy another.'

'So you're going to kill four thousand people instead?'

'No. Only ten. The rest will merely drift, frozen. They'll overshoot their target and carry on forever through the stars. Nobody who ever knew them will ever know. And in a hundred years or so, if others try to make the journey expecting to find a colony, they'll find no trace of the *Owen* or its crew. Clements never knew it was I who helped her aboard, and the staff at the L5 spaceport never knew where she was going. There's no record that she ever came here, and there'll be no evidence of what happened after she arrived. It will be the perfect mystery.'

'Why are you telling me this?' Blair gripped the axe, ready to swing, sure that this was all part of some kind of ruse.

Lambert laughed. 'I suppose I wanted just one person to know what I'd accomplished. What a sacrifice I made.'

Blair waited, but Lambert made no move. Taking one hand off the axe for a moment, Blair touched the handle of the screwdriver sticking out of his flesh. He shuddered. Unable to rush Lambert and the magnetic anchor, all he could do was wait to ambush him beneath the hatch. Yet at the same time, all Lambert had to do was wait for him to tire. This standoff continued for a minute or two before Blair considered a third possibility: one that was certainly not in his favour.

Blair turned on the radio in his helmet. 'Owen, where is Lambert now?'

There was no response.

Considering that Owen might refuse to answer questions about Lambert specifically, Blair tried something harmless: 'Owen, what time is it?'

Nothing. Either Lambert had convinced Owen to ignore Blair completely, or – more likely – he had shut the computer down altogether.

As quietly as possible, Blair released the air from his suit and neck dam, allowing him to turn his head more freely. Then, hearing no response from Lambert, he tucked the head of the axe through the straps of his life support pack. Trusting the helmet to provide at least some protection, he clambered one-handed onto the floor above.

There was nobody there.

Hurriedly, though with great difficulty, Blair pulled himself up the last rungs of the ladder. He retrieved his axe. Lambert was almost certainly trying to circle around him from below.

Though it now had light and power, the ship felt even more threatening than before. So much had depended on uncovering the murderer but, now that Blair had identified him for certain, he found himself injured and alone. Before, he had been faced with a group of suspects, knowing that there was a killer amongst them. Now, he was faced only with empty hallways, and the knowledge that Lambert waited somewhere within.

Beyond the hum of electricity and the wash of liquid through pipes, the ship was silent. Here on the upper level there were no suspension tanks lining the walls. The rooms and equipment on this floor would not see use until the ship arrived in orbit around their destination, and the crew began to ready the new planet for human habitation. Blair passed through quietly, moving from doorway to doorway, hoping that when he found Lambert – or Lambert found him – it wouldn't be out in the open.

There was a faint ring of metal on metal. Instinctively, Blair ducked into the storeroom next to him. The sound immediately brought to mind the heavy magnetic anchor, perhaps striking a rung of the ladder to this floor. Lambert – if it was Lambert that he'd heard – was not close, but still Blair didn't want to risk looking out along the corridor. His only chance to overpower Lambert was by surprise. But Lambert knew that, and time was on his side. Blair doubted the man who had engineered this entire situation could be caught unawares by someone merely hiding behind a door frame.

Blair approached one of the large metal cabinets and tried the door, careful not to make a sound. Sure enough, it was locked. This room housed the few personal possessions that passengers had paid to bring along on their vast journey, dead weight in a place where every gram had to be justified. Anything important enough to make the trip would be bound to make it under lock and key. Blair brought his hand away from the latch, and realised that the glove of his suit was wet with blood. He looked back towards the doorway, noticing for the first time the bloody footprints he'd left on his way through the ship. He wasn't merely being hunted: he was being tracked. Already, Lambert must be following, must be making his way to this very room, and there was nowhere else to hide.

Blair took a step towards the door, but went no farther. The smear of blood on the cabinet caught his attention once more. If he'd entertained the notion that the door might have been unlocked, then so might Lambert.

Blair took off his helmet and pushed it out of sight between two cabinets nearby, leaving just the edge of the gold-tinted visor protruding from the gap. Then, careful not to put his bloodied foot on the floor away from the cabinet he had already marked, he stepped farther into the room, hiding at the end of a row of lockers. There, he waited.

Lambert's approach was silent. Blair's only warning was a flicker of movement in the helmet's reflective visor. Blair himself remained perfectly still, axe clutched tight, his hands trembling. For what seemed like an eternity, Lambert remained nothing more than a distorted shape in the glass, a still figure in the doorway. Then, he stepped forward. Blair held his breath, the shaft of the screwdriver searing as his muscles tensed. There was a rattle of metal as Lambert tried the cabinet, a rush of air as Blair struck.

Lambert wheeled round, lurching backwards as Blair swung. The axe, instead of burying itself in his back, caught him across the knuckle, sending the magnetic anchor crashing into a nearby locker. Fighting the pain in his shoulder as much as Lambert himself, Blair whipped the axe back, striking with the back of the blade like the head of a hammer. Lambert stepped out of the way, the axe caving in the door of a cabinet. Blair, exhausted, swung again, but this time Lambert darted forwards, catching the shaft of the axe with both hands. The two of them toppled to the floor.

Blair found himself flat on his back, the shaft of the axe pressing on his throat, Lambert's entire weight behind it. He tried to push him off, but didn't have the strength. The screwdriver had been knocked in the struggle, and his desperate efforts to escape were only making things worse.

'I had to stop this.' Lambert was almost apologetic. 'If we reach that planet, we'll destroy it. We'll use it up and abandon it, just like Earth. I had to stop it.'

Head twisted at a painful angle, Blair found himself staring into the cabinet he'd struck, the bent door hanging open. Bizarrely, a small bronze bear stared back, looming out of a custom-sized compartment lined with foam. It was a statue – a heavy statue – brought from Earth at considerable expense. Someone frozen on board had chosen to take this statue with them. They'd wanted it as a reminder of Earth: if not for them, then for their children. He reached up, closing his fingers over the bear. He heaved it off the shelf and into the side of Lambert's head.

Lambert rolled sideways, stunned. Struggling to raise himself even to a crouch, Blair brought the bronze bear down once more, favouring the pointed, rigid corner of its base. Lambert's skull yielded beneath the weight.

One

Blair shuffled back through the corridors of the ship, clutching the bronze bear like a talisman. He dropped it down the hatch to the lower floor, climbed through himself, then picked it up from the blood that had pooled around Clements' corpse. He carried it through into Computing Hub Five, to the terminal between the bodies of Aldrin and McConnell, and set it down by the little screen.

Blair felt tired, cold. He supposed that once he had the computer running again, Owen would be able to freeze him, to request that a medical team be present when he was finally defrosted. But after what he'd done to Aldrin, to Clements, even to Lambert, he wasn't sure he cared. It was Lambert who'd started this, but they'd all had a hand in what had happened next, and Blair more than most. Struggling to concentrate, he ran through the process to restart the computer, and was greeted by a slowly filling progress bar as the mainframe performed its customary self-check.

Blair picked up the bronze bear once more. It was a fine piece of art. A fine thing to bring to a new world. A fine artefact of Earth for those who had never seen it for themselves.

He turned the bear over and found a hollow space running up through the base, an effect of the casting process. Inside were sheaves of paper, carefully folded. Blair tugged them out and found valuations, insurance information, a guarantee of authenticity.

A fine investment.

The progress bar filled, the test completed. In its place appeared two options: 'Abort' and 'Continue.'

Blair set the bear down and made his choice.

Murder by Magnetism

There was something magical about an island – the mere word suggested fantasy. You lost touch with the world – an island was a world
of its own. A world, perhaps, from which you might never return.

– And Then There Were None

In space, no one can hear you scream.

– Alien

I wrote *Ten Little Astronauts* for much the same reason that Agatha
Christie wrote *And Then There Were None*: it was a challenge.
Christie's mystery revolves around a small, isolated cast of characters
being gradually picked off by a murderer in their midst, with the
killer's identity remaining unknown even as the number of potential
suspects becomes ever smaller. I wanted to take those basic elements
and try to condense that same sense of fear and tension into a much
shorter story. The interstellar setting was a big part of what made that
possible. Stranded in deep space, it is immediately obvious why the
crew of the U.N. *Owen* cannot count on outside assistance and instead
have to identify the murderer entirely on their own, but having all the
action take place on board a spacecraft will inevitably raise some further questions.

Many people are familiar with the words of Sherlock Holmes in
The Sign of Four: 'When you have eliminated the impossible, whatever
remains, however improbable, must be the truth.' This poses a problem for speculative fiction because the further a story diverges from
everyday reality, the harder it becomes to distinguish between what
might be possible and what isn't. There is generally an expectation
that when reading a murder mystery, it should be possible – at least in
theory – to work out whodunnit before the answer is revealed on the
page. Christie's own mystery plots frequently draw upon her background in pharmacology and sometimes hinge upon details that the
average reader would not know already, but someone with the necessary knowledge may well pick up on them. For these reasons, it

seemed only sensible to make *Ten Little Astronauts* a work of hard science fiction, in which the reality of the book conforms as closely as possible to our own. This more or less ruled out teleportation, force-fields, faster-than-light travel, and a variety of other sci-fi staples.

With the exception of the 'suspension tanks' used to hold the crew in a frozen state, the technologies on board the U.N. *Owen* are achievable – some even unremarkable – today. The futuristic-sounding ion thrusters were developed in the 1960s and have already been used to propel the *Dawn* spacecraft to Ceres (and also to adjust the orbits of numerous satellites around Earth). The first working coilgun (described at the time as an 'electromagnetic cannon') was built over a hundred years ago, and versions adapted from household electronics are popular hobby projects today. The chemical oxygen generators that sustain the crew are the same as those fitted in commercial aircraft in case of loss of cabin pressure.

The overall ambiance of the ship was inspired by HMS *Alliance* at the Royal Navy Submarine Museum (which also very kindly allowed me to film the promotional video for *Ten Little Astronauts* on board). Though something like Mir or the International Space Station might seem more directly comparable, both are very small. I was working from the idea that a vessel designed to reach even the closest neighbouring star would have to be truly enormous, if for no other reason than to carry enough reaction mass to propel it. From that point of view, HMS *Alliance* was a much better match.

A faster-than-light ship might be a stretch too far for a murder mystery, but at a certain point a ship travelling significantly slower than light becomes just as implausible. At the time of writing, only one human-made object – the *Voyager 1* probe – has entered interstellar space, and it took nearly four decades to get there. To not only leave our solar system but reach another one, the *Owen* would have to be travelling at a substantial fraction of the speed of light to make the trip in anything less than several hundred years (which would raise questions about what could possibly power the ship and how it could run for so long without oversight or maintenance).

My desire for scientific accuracy led to some interesting discoveries while writing. Much of what's commonly believed about space is surprisingly inaccurate. Exposure to a vacuum will not cause the human body to burst open (though it's still best avoided for plenty of other reasons), and the space between stars is not a total vacuum either. This poses another problem for anyone who wants to pass through it, since at the sort of relativistic speed you would have to be travelling to get anywhere, the stationary molecules of gas you run into along the way behave exactly the same as relativistic particles running into you. The difference between the two is a little like the difference between tripping onto a javelin and having the thing thrown at you, except that in this scenario either you or the javelin is moving at 90,000 kilometres a second.

Comparatively little of what I discovered made it into *Ten Little Astronauts* in the end – a large part of the challenge in writing the book was telling the story without getting bogged down in the scientific details – but the elements that do appear have been very carefully selected. However, I don't think this is the only way to construct a mystery in a sci-fi setting. The following story, *Six Years Stolen*, offers one alternative. I hope you enjoy it.

Six Years Stolen

'Blue, please.'

The man at the kiosk drops a brick of noodles into the blue compartment and shuts the lid. There's a steady hiss as the machine forces a torrent of boiling water through the sieve, then a rising whine as the cooking phase ends and the centrifuge spins the noodles to reclaim the excess moisture. Finally, the compartment pops open, producing a thick cloud of steam pungent with synthetic spice.

The cook – hand wrapped in a threadbare towel – lifts the sieve from the machine and dumps the noodles in a blue plastic bowl.

'Seventeen fifty.'

I press my thumb to the reader and he passes me the noodles.

It's nearly 5am and all the seats are taken. I join a group standing beneath the tarpaulins stretched between the street lamps, listening to the rain pounding the PVC and trying not to let the drips fall in my food.

Outside, a constable trudges pointlessly across the empty square, his gloves duct-taped to his sleeves. He catches me staring and he nods. I can't tell who it is past the mask and goggles, but I nod back anyway.

Someone gets up from a table near the edge of the shelter, and I seize my chance. As I do so, there's a commotion at the kiosk.

'I've got money – your machine's broken!'

Before I can stop myself, I'm looking back. There's a man wrapped in bin bags at the front of the queue. He's got no money and the machine works fine.

The guy in the kiosk turns to me: 'Are you gonna do anything about this?'

The homeless man turns too, grey hair plastered to his swollen face. His eyes are running and his skin is red.

'It's my day off.' I wave a hand towards the square. 'My colleague would be happy to help.'

Fortunately that's all it takes.

'No need.' The man puts up his sodden hood. 'I'll be taking my business elsewhere.'

I turn back to the table with the empty seat, but that seat's not empty any more. I'm not even sure which one it was. I glare at the plastic-swathed figure as he slinks away, but he's already hurrying for the entrance of someplace he definitely can't afford to shop.

I stare at the officer in the square, willing him to catch the vagrant out, but he doesn't. He simply keeps shambling along, sub-machine gun hanging from its sling and thumping wetly against the front of his raincoat with every step.

My noodles are cooling rapidly. I've eaten half before another seat opens up. The second half is cold.

I blow my entertainment budget on a ticket to the opening of *Citizen Kane* after lunch, and immediately regret my decision. The image is flickery and grainy, and has no colour. Posters in the foyer declare it a return to an earlier style of filmmaking, but this is mere propaganda: the entertainment industry has been cutting corners ever since the start of the War.

By the time the crowd spills from the theatre, it has gone seven. The constable I saw in the square is still around, still in uniform, still unrecognisable. I wave anyway. The constable raises a hand in reply, then topples to the concrete just beside a parked van. I wait for him to stand.

He doesn't.

I walk over to where the constable lies slumped over the curb, face down in the rush of water flowing to the drain. The water as it flows to meet him is clear. The water as it flows away is red.

'Get away from there! Run!'

There's another constable on the scene, but he isn't doing anything. He's just kneeling in a doorway, yelling at me.

'He needs an ambulance!' I yell back. 'Call an ambulance!'

I lift the fallen constable's head from the flooded gutter, feeling something yield beneath the hood. I pull it back.

There is a crater the size of my fist in the man's skull.

'We need that ambulance!' I shout. 'Call—'

I look up just in time to see the constable from the doorway charging towards me, revolver in hand. But rather than firing, he simply barrels into me and we both crash into the side of the van before tumbling to the ground.

I fight back, elbowing him on the nose as I make a grab for the weapon. Something buzzes through the air.

There is a bang, but it is not the revolver. I feel a rush of air against my face, escaping from the van's burst tyre.

The constable grabs at the collar of my coat, apparently unaware of the nosebleed I've given him. 'This way! Quick!'

I follow him back to the doorway. He kicks the door twice, unsuccessfully, before unloading his revolver into the wood next to the handle and shouldering his way through. I step inside after him and find that we have broken into a narrow, windowless stairwell where he slumps down on the steps. He drops his gun and retrieves the radio from his belt.

He thumbs the button to transmit: 'Block Six. One officer down. Send the response team in from the north side: the sniper's got a view of the theatre.'

***

'All right, Malcolm.' Superintendent Cowell adjusts the voice recorder on his desk. 'Tell me everything you remember.'

'I was off duty,' I protest.

'Whether you were on duty or off duty doesn't matter,' he says, already exasperated. 'You were present. That means you might have seen something that may prove relevant. Now. Tell me everything you remember.'

'I...' I wonder how far back he wants me to start. The homeless man at the noodle bar? The subpar movie?

Cowell watches me, his brow furrowed and his patience strained.

'I saw another constable,' I begin. 'I waved at him and he fell on the ground. Then I went over and there was a lot of blood. That was when I saw the other constable: I told him to call an ambulance but he knocked me over instead.'

I pause. It occurs to me that, though strictly accurate, my account of events might not be entirely fair.

'I think he was trying to help me,' I add. 'We broke down the door of a building and when we were inside he called for backup. We stayed there and a helicopter came and then I had to come here. That's everything I know.'

Cowell sighs. Slowly, lethargically, he opens the drawer of his desk and takes out a foil-covered box. He shakes out a cigarette – platinum-rated, each one worth ten bowls of noodles – and puts it in his mouth.

'Malcolm…' the cigarette dangles from his lip as he brings up the lighter, 'we're not getting anywhere.'

'Sorry,' I mumble.

He takes a big breath of smoke, sweeping some loose flakes of tobacco from his immaculately polished desk as he does so.

I wait as he breathes out, inspects the tip of his cigarette, rubs his eyes with a yellowed hand.

'There's one more thing we can do. I've got a health industry consultant here to see you.'

'But I feel fine.'

'I know. It's… I'll let her explain.'

Before I can protest, he's pushed a button on his desk. A buzzer sounds in the room outside, and a moment later the consultant steps in.

'Hello,' she says, smiling. 'I'm Doctor Galer. Your employer tells me you intend to withdraw from some medication.'

'What? No.'

'Just give him the basics, Doctor.'

'What's going on?' I demand.

She looks at me – obviously more clueless than she anticipated – then turns back to Cowell. 'I think you're in a better position to explain that than I am, Superintendent.'

'Very well.' Cowell takes another drag on his cigarette before addressing me: 'I want to promote you. In a manner of speaking. I'm offering you a position as a sleeper agent. But this position has certain… medical requirements.'

He looks back to Galer, who grudgingly speaks: 'As you may know, every citizen is administered with regular doses of phoebusine.

The drug has been in constant use for more than a century, generally recognised as safe, non-addictive and side-effect free.'

I didn't know that. Didn't even know I'd been taking it. 'What? Why? What will happen if I stop?'

'For a few hours, nothing. A little longer, and your reflexes and mental agility would suffer. Then, you would lose consciousness.' Noticing my concern, she adds: 'Temporarily, of course. After a day or two, you'd be back to your usual self.'

'Then...' The question is obvious. 'Why is everybody taking the drug?'

'That loss of consciousness would not be an isolated event. Without phoebusine, you would black out for six to nine hours every day.'

There's an awkward silence. It seems more awkward for Cowell than for Galer and me.

'The blackouts are actually a natural phenomenon known in medical circles as "sleep". This was once experienced by virtually every human on Earth, and can still be observed in animals today.'

'But why?' I ask.

'Quite simply, we don't know. The widespread adoption of phoebusine was responsible for the single biggest increase in industrial productivity in history. The benefits of sleep are trivial in comparison to the time it robs us of. However, those who regularly partake in it do show somewhat heightened mental capacity.'

'Which is why it would be useful to us here,' puts in Cowell. 'Though you don't think you know any useful information about the sniper, you might have witnessed something that would prove critical to our investigation if you were better able to recognise its significance. Sleeper agents are those within the security industry who are not treated with phoebusine, and instead spend around a third of their time in sleep in order to bolster their lateral thinking skills and hopefully identify connections that other employees might overlook. Your presence at the scene today makes you a promising candidate.'

He crushes the remains of his cigarette against the sole of his shoe and drops it in the bin. 'That guy killed a constable. We didn't get him this time, and in all likelihood he'll strike again.' He gives me a significant look. 'Without you, even more lives might be lost.'

'I don't know...' I have my doubts. Healthy people don't faint every day.

'I thought you might say that, so I arranged for someone else to meet you.'

Again the button. Again the buzzer. A familiar figure steps through the door.

'Hello.' He puts out his hand for me to shake, but doesn't smile.

Cowell, however, does. 'You met Inspector Burford earlier today. He's a sleeper agent: his superior reflexes may well have saved you.'

'Thanks,' I say.

'Don't mention it.' He wrinkles his swollen nose.

'So...' Cowell ignores the cold introduction. 'Got any advice for Malcolm here?'

'Try to make sure you're lying down when it happens,' says Burford. 'Galer calls it "falling asleep" for a reason.'

'Would I be able to start taking phoebusine again?' I ask her.

'With a little difficulty,' she explains. 'Though the drug is not addictive, the biological processes it suppresses appear to be. Most people who withdraw from phoebusine do not choose to begin using it again.'

I see myself in ten years' time: addicted to sleep, my life wasting away before my closed eyes.

'I'm sorry. I don't think I can do this.' I stand up and turn to leave.

'I didn't want to say this,' sighs Superintendent Cowell, 'but if you walk out of that door, you're fired.'

I stop, one leg still hooked awkwardly around the chair.

'Constable Gareth McCall has been killed. Inspector Burford was lucky to survive his attempt to pull you from the scene. Do you think I can let you walk out of here if there's even the slightest chance you can stop this happening again?'

I think back to that moment and suddenly I know what Cowell is about to say.

'There were a hundred people coming out of that theatre – it would have been impossible not to hit one in the crowd – yet he went for the lone policeman across the road. Then he targeted you and Burford. Why do you think that might have been?' The Superintendent rattles another cigarette out of the pack and lights it with shaking hands. 'We searched every inch of every building with a view of the site where McCall was killed. Do you know what we found?'

He takes a drag. I'm not sure if he's waiting for me to answer or just steadying his nerves.

'Nothing. No casings. No broken glass. No open windows. Nothing. This isn't some kid with a gun: it's a trained sniper, and he's after the police.'

There is a pause while Cowell collects himself.

It is Burford who breaks the silence: 'Sleeper agents are usually chosen through highly selective screening and psychometric tests. Frankly, fielding someone as unqualified as you would be a disgrace to the industry. But the Superintendent feels that if you get results then you'll have proved your worth. If not...' he shrugs. 'You can always go back to herding the homeless.'

Cowell ashes his cigarette into the bin. 'Thank you, Burford. You may go. Chase Ballistics for that report: I want it on my desk the moment it's available.'

'Yes, Superintendent.'

Burford leaves, pulling the door closed behind him. Galer remains, watching.

'So,' says Cowell. 'What'll it be?'

I think about his offer. Not so much about the job itself, but about my small room in Headquarters. My clothes. My shoes. My health insurance and food allowance. My entertainment budget. My pension. The industry owns all these things. If I lose my job, I lose them too. Then what? If I'm lucky, a few days on the streets between jobs. If I'm not, the rest of my life: a year or two at most.

'Okay. I'll do it.' I don't have a choice.

'That's the spirit,' says Cowell, flatly.

'I'll need to remove your subcutaneous delivery system,' explained Galer. 'It's not healthy to keep one fitted empty.'

'Is that difficult?'

'It's very minor surgery. The sort of thing that's routinely done before an MRI. Installing a new one is marginally more troublesome, but we'll cross that bridge when we come to it.'

***

I try to ignore the thick, yellow fluid oozing from my sternum. I try also to ignore the small army of doctors bustling about, and the standby defibrillator by my bed. Professor Galer looms over me, doing absolutely nothing to put me at ease.

'It's been two hours now,' she says, slowly, as though I am a child. 'We've seen withdrawal affect patients this early a few times before, so it's important that you remember to remain calm.'

This conversation is doing nothing to help.

'It won't be sudden: you'll lose consciousness by degrees. Don't resist it. Remember that the first time is not typical. You could remain unconscious for days. On subsequent occasions it'll be far less severe, and for just a few hours. So don't worry.'

The only thing worse than my concern over things going wrong is Galer's insistence that I not worry about things going wrong.

'Can I get some water?' I ask, partly because I'm thirsty but mostly to get Galer to leave me alone for a minute.

'Joe?' she looks to one of the nurses before turning back to me. 'Would you mind?'

I close my eyes in frustration. When I open them, Galer is gone.

I lie still for a moment, feeling very tired and generally awful. The prospect of slipping into a coma is looking significantly more and more welcome, but I do hope I'll at least get a drink first.

I see Joe in the doorway, but he's just passing by. I wonder if he's forgotten, or if he's just fobbed the job off on someone else.

'Hey,' I call. Or try to, because all I can manage is a croak.

'You'll want your water,' says Galer, who it turns out merely moved to a chair in the corner of the room.

'Yeah.'

'It's there.' She points out the table by my bed.

'That was quick,' I say, taking a sip and immediately feeling marginally less bad.

'It was,' she agrees, 'but it's been there since Thursday.'

My stomach lurches. 'What time is it now?'

'Nine twenty-five, Saturday morning. You came through very well.'

I take another sip, not entirely confident that this isn't a joke. I'm half relieved to have made it through the ordeal so easily, half terrified to know that I am now definitely prone to these attacks. I think of all the work I might have done since Thursday afternoon. Even if it won't be so long in future, those hours will add up.

'How long will it be normally?'

'It varies from person to person, but you can expect it to be somewhere in the region of eight hours per day.'

Twenty-four divided by eight. Three. I would be spending a third of my remaining lifetime unconscious. For every three days Galer lived, I would only see two.

'Can I go for a walk?' I ask.

She thinks for a moment. 'Yes, but take it easy. If you feel tired or dizzy, sit – or better, lie down – and tell a member of staff. On second thoughts, I'll come with you. I'm the only somnologist here.'

I find myself unsteady on my feet, but not altogether bad. Maybe it's just the extra days off, but I feel refreshed, if also a little achy. I make my way slowly to a window and look down at the road. It's still dark – the sun isn't yet high enough to reach the street below – and it's raining hard. I think for a moment that it's been raining a long time, then realise that the shower falling when I stepped inside the hospital must doubtless have cleared sometime in the past two days.

'Can't it wait?'

I turn. Doctor Galer is talking to a sergeant I've seen around Headquarters from time to time. He's making more of an effort to keep his voice down than she is – I don't catch his response – but I hear Galer's words clearly.

'I don't care what the Superintendent says! He's my patient, and I'll see to it that...'

She's noticed me watching.

'Very well.' She glares at the sergeant. 'Since it would probably only cause more distress to keep it from him now, I will inform your colleague.' She walks over to me, speaking more quietly: 'There's been another attack.'

'Is anyone...' I can't quite manage the word.

'More than one.'

My face must show my guilt, because she places a hand awkwardly on my shoulder. 'Look, you're probably doing more good here than you would have—'

'I know!' I snap. 'That's the problem.'

***

Inspector Burford is at the scene when I arrive, hard to recognise in his rain gear. The bodies lie beneath polyester tents.

Burford nods at the flimsy structures. 'Got them up as quickly as we could, though most of the damage has been done.'

It's quite a downpour. Holding my hood in place, I look up, pretending to check the sky. Really I'm more interested in the windows overlooking us.

'He'll be long gone by now, though the buildings are still locked down. We've got half a dozen response teams making a sweep.'

I clear the raindrops from my goggles. 'Any idea where he was shooting from?'

'Best guess is between ten and fifteen floors up from somewhere over there. The rain has washed away a lot of the blood spatter, so we can't know for sure.'

'I thought there were machines...' I stammer. 'Can't they work it out from the sound of the gunshot?'

'Only if there is a gunshot.'

Burford produces a small plastic bag from the pocket of his raincoat. Inside is a long, dented metal object.

'This was recovered from the scene on Thursday. It's one of the bullets. Notice anything unusual?'

I squint at the projectile. Even through my smeared goggles and the misty plastic bag, one thing stands out clearly: 'It's pointed at both ends.'

'That's because it never had to fit into a casing. This is coilgun ammunition. The innovation industry confirmed it.'

'What's a—'

'A coilgun doesn't use gunpowder. It uses electromagnets. These things are almost completely silent.'

'So how do we find the shooter?'

'By tracking down the gun. They're still in limited initial production: only a few hundred have ever been made. It's almost certain that the sniper is a veteran of the Congo war.'

'So we're looking for a Congolese soldier?'

'More likely one of our own.' Burford sighs. 'The Congo doesn't have anything like this kind of technology.' There's something in his voice just then.

'You don't... sympathise with them, do you?'

'No, of course not. But still...' he glances around before speaking. 'The more you shut your eyes, the more you'll see.'

We stand in silence for a minute, surveying the scene. There's really not much else to do.

Finally, Burford speaks once more: 'Assuming it's a single shooter, we're probably looking for someone among the homeless. With two attacks in one week, they can't be in employment: their absence would be noted. I doubt any of our informants will be able to identify the sniper himself, but they can point us to the current dissident leaders. That'll be a start. Even if we can't find the puppet, perhaps we'll be able to cut the strings.'

There is a rat in the street. Not unusual in itself – there have been rats everywhere since the sanitation industry's poisons stopped working – but this particular rat is very strange indeed. Its fur is a pearly, ghostly white, so light that the concrete beneath its paws seems to glow. It stares at me through bulging, pink eyes.

I raise a foot, ready to crush the rat, but before I can stamp down there is a squeal. I move my foot aside to see, and the rat is convulsing, its teeth set into an electrical cable lying in the road. I attempt to nudge it away with my shoe, but the current spreads up my leg, making every muscle in my body spasm.

'Malcolm.' Burford is shaking me. 'Malcolm.'

I look over at him, feeling upholstery against my back once again, and the familiar pull and wheel of the moving car.

'What happened?' I ask.

'You fell asleep. It is a little late.'

'But what about...'

I try to remember what I had been thinking about before. We had been outside.

I don't feel right. 'What time is it?'

'Eleven thirty-ish.'

'That's crazy! I've only been working...' I counted, '... fourteen hours!'

'Give it a few days, and that'll feel like a lot more.'

'We're wasting so much time!'

'Haven't you seen *Blade Runner*?'

I had, once, when it had come out a couple of years ago. I didn't see why it was relevant now.

'The candle that burns twice as bright burns half as long.'

I glance at him to see if he's joking. He isn't.

We return to headquarters, and I return to my room.

There is a bed here now, with a pole to hold a drip just like in the hospital. My desk and chair have been crammed up against the wall to make space for the thing.

I lie down in case of sleep, but soon find myself in the street once more, examining the cable. There is a dog now, thrashing in the current with the frayed wire in its mouth. Its short tail is curled back against its spine.

***

My watch alarm sounds, and I discover that almost seven hours have passed without my knowledge. I swing my legs over the edge of the bed and spend one more minute trying to piece together my movements during that time.

It is impossible. All I can recall is that at some point I left my room, and sometime after that I must have returned.

My skin feels hot. My head is pounding. I realise I must have slept, that this must be interfering with my memory of the time before, but still the knowledge is unsettling. I stumble to the sink and drink from the tap. I splash some water on my face. I stand with my fingers closed over the cool steel rim of the basin, wondering if the knot in my stomach is merely stress or I really am about to vomit.

The phone on my desk begins to ring. I check my watch and find that four further minutes have passed unnoticed.

I slip out of the door and hurry down the stairs.

'You're late,' says Superintendent Cowell as I push open the meeting room door. Burford is already inside, pouring himself a cup of burnt-smelling coffee.

I try to force out some excuse, and settle on 'Sorry.' My mouth feels fuzzy, like mouldy bread.

'The reports are in,' he continues, ignoring my apology. 'Though we have no clear suspect at this time, the innovation industry has helped us narrow down the options somewhat. They've been uncharacteristically forthcoming about the weapon involved in these shootings.'

He slides a file towards me across the long conference table. A slim stack of schematics protrudes from the open edge as it comes to a stop, and a couple of glossy photographs slip out entirely. I pick one up. The image is of a woman in a boiler suit holding up what appears to be a length of guttering.

'The gun isn't what you might expect,' explains Cowell. 'Quite simply, without the stock and sight attached you wouldn't recognise it as a weapon. The thing's made of plastic. Besides the trigger it's got no moving parts. Anyone could hide it, and anyone could use it. However...'

He walks over and presses a finger to the other photo, lying on the table.

'Most of the electronics are housed in this external pack. Even vehicle-mounted, with the engine to top up the power, that's twenty kilos of equipment. On foot, provided he expects more than one shot, our sniper is carrying upwards of fifty. That will attract attention and it gives us some idea who we're looking for: most likely a man, and definitely someone larger than average.'

'We've got the beginnings of a criminal profile too,' says Burford. 'Everything about the attacks suggests the offender has a military background. Four of the five shots fired so far hit their target, and he's managed to remain entirely undetected on two separate occasions. It's possible that's only because he's attacked at long range and given us a wide area to search, but that would still suggest we're dealing with an experienced sharpshooter.'

'Does that narrow it down enough for us to bring anybody in?' I ask.

'Not on its own,' says Cowell. 'We're still waiting for the peace industry to put together a report. Burford believes we're looking for a veteran of the Congo War, most likely a designated marksman, probably discharged in the past few weeks. But it's little more than guesswork at this stage.'

Burford sets down his coffee. 'That report is our best chance of ending this. First we detain anyone who could carry out another attack, then we determine who was responsible for the two we've seen already. Until then, all we can do is circulate these photographs and hope somebody recognises the weapon.'

'The attacks will not be made public.'

Burford leans forward. 'Sir, I understand why you'd prefer to keep this within the industry, but it's vastly more likely that we'll see results if—'

'Neither will this information be released internally.'

The room is silent, besides a faint electrical hum from the coffee maker.

After a brief pause, Cowell returns to the file on the table. 'Our priority right now will be to process surveillance footage from—'

'No, hang on. Do you mean to tell me that you're not doing anything about this? That you're sending officers out with no idea about the sniper?'

'The most important thing is not to cause a panic.' Cowell's voice is firm. 'Above all else, the security industry must maintain order. Our officers can't do that if they're afraid to go out on the streets.'

'Will you at least issue ballistic vests?'

'That gun fires solid steel rounds. It would make Kevlar look like cling film.'

I feel as though I should say something, but I don't know what.

'Our most pressing concern,' Cowell continues, 'is examining the footage collected from buildings overlooking—'

Burford speaks again: 'I just think—'

'It is not your job to think about the safety of our personnel!' snaps Cowell. 'It is mine. And that job would be much easier if you could focus on the task at hand.'

'Yes, sir.' Burford stares into his coffee. 'Sorry, sir.'

***

There are hours of footage to scour. Hours for each camera. And there are many cameras.

Every recording of the attacks themselves has been examined and re-examined, but still Burford insists on watching them again. I see the shooting that happened while I was asleep. One officer drops to the ground, the reason unclear. Another hurries over – just as I had done – and soon falls too. The third is killed off-frame: in the same street, but not witnessed by this camera. Not one of them knew the danger.

Burford brings up another recording, the low-resolution image smeared across the polished glass. Even pixelated, through the water-stained lens of the theatre's CCTV, I recognise myself in the crowd that spills into the screen. I see myself raise an arm and the other officer fall. I see myself move over. Throughout it all, the crowd remains as oblivious as I was.

Then heads begin to turn. I wonder why until I realise that this must have been the moment Burford shouted. This footage has no sound. A few seconds pass and I see myself stoop to touch the fallen constable, see Burford break into a run. I see the van drop slightly as a steel bullet slices through its tyre. From this angle I can just make out a spray of grit as the projectile emerges, glancing against the concrete like a stone skipping over water. The crowd simply watches. Not a single person turns away. Not a single person runs.

'Sorry,' I say to Burford, not quite able to take my eyes off the screen.

'That's alright. You don't get far in this job if you can't take a punch.'

'No.' I realise with a twinge of guilt that I'd forgotten that I hit him. 'I mean about before. About Cowell. I should have backed you up.'

'Should have shut me up, more like.'

'What?'

'He's wrong about the photographs. About keeping this quiet. But you can't convince him, and it's not a good idea to try.'

'But he brought you on as an expert. He—'

'He brought me on to supervise you. Cowell doesn't understand our work. He thinks that if we sift through enough evidence, one of us will have some kind of premonition. He doesn't realise that we could be coordinating the search. Doctor Galer's tried to get through to him so many times but he can't grasp it and I don't think…'

Burford sighs, pausing the video that neither of us are watching.

'I don't think she can explain. She's brilliant, but she's tired. Everybody's tired.'

There's a pause. I get the feeling he thinks that nothing more needs to be said, but I'm just trying to work out what he means. I'm exhausted. He looks exhausted. But back in the meeting room, Cowell was the same as ever. I was never this tired before I had to sleep.

'Could you explain it yourself?' I ask, more to break the silence than anything else.

'I tried a few times. A long time ago. Think it did more harm than good. It doesn't matter how well you make the case: when it's you making it, you're just another employee asking for a better pay package.'

'Well…' I feel as though I should console him but I'm not sure how. I shrug. 'What can you do?'

He takes it as a serious question. 'All you can do: keep your head down, pay your dues, and maybe someday work your way up to a position where you can actually make a difference.' He resumes the video. 'It's as good a reason as any for putting in the work now.'

***

Days pass before the peace industry's report arrives. Burford and I spend them poring over the same files, the same footage, except for the four hours we spend out in the rain, watching Forensics try to piece together what evidence they can from the latest victim while ten separate squads lock down every building with a view of the site. When we return, the report has been waiting for two-and-a-half hours.

'They've included a very comprehensive list of all employees with access to a coilgun. Naturally their movements are easily accounted for, as are those weapons, and thus we can eliminate them from our investigation.' Cowell dumps a large sheaf of papers unceremoniously on the farthest corner of the meeting room table. 'The information on those they've discharged is considerably more sparse.'

I glance through the documents. Each one follows the same basic format: there's a name, a position within the industry, a photo. Some list a new occupation, but more – many more – simply note that the individual is no longer an employee.

'Any with a known address we'll hold immediately,' says Cowell. 'We'll just have to hope the teams sweeping the streets can identify the others.'

I make my way down the road, knowing that I should be looking for something but somehow not able to remember what. In the distance, a dog barks. A rat darts out from beneath a van. Just as quickly, it vanishes into a drain set into the curb.

Somebody is watching me as I watch the rat. I try to scan the windows overhead, but the moment I look up I realise that I have neglected to put my goggles on. I lower my head, pulling my hood down to protect my eyes. Then, at last, I see it: the cable in the gutter.

'You've witnessed something that may prove critical to our investigation,' says Cowell, not looking up from the documents in front of him. 'You just don't recognise its significance.'

I stare at the cable a moment longer, stoop to grasp it, bring it to my mouth. The rubbery taste of the plastic insulation meets my tongue. I bite down. Lightning flashes through my teeth and into my bones. I fall to the ground and lie there convulsing, the surface of the concrete grinding into my cheek. Cowell remains sitting at his desk. Still he does not look up.

The car stops. I peel my face from the inside of the window and try to blink away the street lamps' glare. It does very little good.

'Come on,' says Burford, shutting off the engine and opening the door. 'Let's eat somewhere indoors this time. Maybe that silver-rated place on the corner? I think we've earned it.'

I check my watch: 11.17. Outside in the square, the noodle bar stands empty. It's not raining any more, and it's too early for the midnight crowd. There's no sign of the cook, even, unless he's the figure sitting underneath the tarpaulins. I try to piece together where the past few hours went: I remember interviewing suspects, so I can't have been asleep the whole time. I'm still holding a slim stack of profiles, now slightly crumpled.

'Hey!' Burford snaps his fingers a few times. 'You can sleep later. First you need food.'

The figure at the table gets up and walks away. He walks rather quickly. I'm reminded of a swollen face and an argument over a thumb reader. I'm reminded also of a pixelated greyscale photo.

'Hey!' Burford slaps the dashboard. 'Are—' He notices me rifling through the profiles.

'Stop that man.' I point out the guy moving away from us across the square, now practically running.

Burford lurches from the car and sprints after him. I dump the documents and follow: I still can't match a name to the face, but it doesn't matter now. He knows we're after him. He chose to run.

The man swerves down an alley, then tears open an emergency exit, propped open with a fire extinguisher. He kicks the thing aside. There are screams as he forces his way into the building, tugging the door shut behind him.

'Open up!' yells Burford, banging on it with the butt of his revolver. 'Police! Police!'

By the time somebody pushes it open, I've caught up. The door leads to the kitchen of a restaurant.

'Which way?' demands Burford, but unless the guy is hiding in the freezer I can see there's only one route he could have taken.

I rush through into the restaurant, and though I can't see the suspect, everyone else is looking in the same direction. I run out into the shopping centre the place is attached to and see him shove his way into the back-of-house corridors. If I hadn't seen him open one, I would never have known they were there: I get the feeling he knows the place.

Now it's up to Burford to catch up with me.

'This way!' I shout, drawing my own revolver as I push open the door.

The moment I do, the man is on top of me: one hand on the barrel of my gun, the other thrusting a knife towards my face. Suddenly, bafflingly – despite everything else going through my mind – I am very aware that the blade smells of onions.

Flinching back from the knife, I twist the gun towards his leg and pull the trigger. The bullet misses, but the flash of hot gas escaping between barrel and cylinder blasts across his wrist. He cries out, letting go of the gun. I press it to his chest and fire a second shot.

Burford pushes open the door – weapon at the ready, trying to keep behind the frame as far as he can – but the danger has passed. The suspect lies spread out on the floor, tattered sleeve smouldering, blood just beginning to pool beneath his back. His mouth still twitches but his eyes are still.

'Dudley Ringwald.' The name comes to me, unexpected as the scent of onions. 'Designated marksman.'

***

The shot tears through the plasterboard wall of the meeting room, shattering the jug in the coffee maker. I shrink behind the table, knowing that it won't stop a bullet, not even sure it'll hide me from view. Outside the meeting room, the third-floor windows run floor-to-ceiling from stairwell to stairwell. Across the road, there's another wall of glass. I can feel the sniper's gaze, sense the gunsights tracing across the room. The only sound is my heart thudding against my ribs: I don't hear the shot.

I wake in a panic, and it only gets worse. I try to remind myself that there have been no attacks for two weeks. That the man I killed ticked every box we were looking for. That there's been no evidence of an accomplice. It doesn't help. It isn't the killer that concerns me: it's the visions. Sleeper agents are usually chosen though screening and tests, Cowell had said. I've been through none of that, and the hallucinations are getting more frequent. It's not safe for me to keep going like this, but the only way to stop now is to leave the industry: I can't do that.

I pick up the phone, listen to the clicking static for a moment, then put back it back down again. Burford might be able to help – might – but talking to him on that line would be the same as calling Cowell. I can wait until our next shift. It's not a perfect plan, but it's better than any alternative I can think of with the terror of the vision still fresh in my mind. Burford might reveal my doubts – might use me as a stepping stone to his promotion – but somehow I don't think so. Even if he did, that might end better for me than if I went to Cowell myself.

I lie awake a few minutes more before I find myself back out on the street with the familiar cable, the familiar taste of plastic, the familiar blinding shock. My body lurches in the bed.

***

'I need you to do me a favour,' I say. I've been over this conversation in my head a thousand times, and somehow not once have I come up with anything better than this.

'Okay…' He waits for me to explain.

I wait for a solid 'yes.'

'What is it?' he asks at last. I suppose you don't get far in the industry volunteering for things before you know what they are.

'This work doesn't suit me.' It's the best that I can manage. 'I need you to tell Cowell that you don't need me any more. That you'd find it easier without me.'

There's a brief silence before he answers. I squint, trying to watch his expression despite the sun beaming down into the square, filtered through the thin cloud whiting out the sky. The noodle bar has taken down the groundsheets: it hasn't rained in days.

'I'm not going to do that,' Burford says at last. 'Making it look like I can't work with you won't do me any favours. Not sure it'll do you any either.'

I lean forwards. 'I can't keep going like this. I just can't. I—'

'Then tell Cowell that.'

'I can't! You were there when this began: he won't let me. Not as long as he thinks I can make a difference.'

'You can make a difference. You spotted Dudley Ringwald. You chased him down.' He shrugs. 'You blundered into him like an idiot and cost us any chance of an interview, but I'm not sure we were ever going to take him alive.'

'But I can't do this any more.'

'Why?' Burford puts a hand on the table. 'We took down Ringwald, the shootings stopped. As far as anyone can tell, he was working alone. All that's left is to find the gun, and for all we know it could turn up tomorrow. Why are you so determined to give up now?'

'I never signed up for this. I didn't go through any of the tests. I—'

'I didn't make Inspector by ignoring the obvious. What are you not telling me?'

'I see things when I sleep.' I'm not sure how to explain. 'Things that aren't real. They seem real at the time, but then when I wake up, I realise they weren't. Sometimes. Sometimes I'm not sure.'

Burford sits and watches me a long time. I wonder if I can get my old job – and my phoebusine – back for medical reasons, or if they'll just drop me from the industry. There are always people willing to work security. Always.

'Did Doctor Galer really not tell you about that?'

'No. What does it mean?'

'It doesn't mean anything, Malcolm. They're dreams. You sleep, your brain isn't working on any real problems, it makes stuff up.'

It takes me a moment to realise he's speaking from experience. 'You get that too?'

'Not all the time. But, a lot of the time.' He thinks. 'Six years, Galer says. Six years of dreams in a lifetime. Probably less for us.'

***

I stand by the body, staring into the gaping hole in the neck and willing myself to wake up. But this time I'm not dreaming. I feel a tear of frustration hit the bottom of my goggles and soak into my skin. We didn't stop it. We did nothing. The only reason for the two-week respite was that there was nothing to wash the blood spatter away, nothing to help disguise the direction of the shot. The rain pounds on the polyester overhead.

'Come on,' says Burford. 'We have to check the building.'

We step into the lift and make our way up to the seventeenth floor. There we see it: the first evidence we've had, besides bodies and bullets, that the sniper even exists. It's an open window.

I look out down the street at the scene of the shooting. The tent is a dot. The body must be barely more than a speck. I try and picture how much harder it would be to see the sniper from the ground. A rifle barrel resting in one window – one of ten thousand – seventeen floors up.

'These windows aren't supposed to open that far,' says Burford. 'The killer unscrewed part of the hinge but must not have been able to fix it back in place.'

'I'm not surprised,' I say. 'We had every building with a view of the victim locked down within five minutes. They couldn't have hung about.'

'Why do you say 'they'?' asks Burford. 'You think we might be looking for a woman?'

I shrug. 'Profiling suggests a man, though that's hardly certain. I was thinking more that it might be multiple people. Ringwald definitely wasn't acting alone.'

Burford's eyes are on the tent in the distance. 'I'm beginning to think he might not have been acting at all.'

'What do you mean? He resisted arrest – he tried to kill me – there's no way he was innocent.'

'I'm not so sure that proves anything. Remember I was hoping to get some information out of our informants?'

'No.' If I ever heard anything about that, it hadn't been for a while.

'Turns out they were caught up in one of the sweeps. The industry's been very thorough. At first I thought that might be a bonus – get them to talk to us in exchange for an early release – but I don't think they'll be talking to us at all.'

He hands me a few pages. I look through them. There are half a dozen names.

'I don't know any of them,' I say, offering the pages back.

'No. Look here.' He points out a note attached to each one: 'Transferred to Portland Yard.'

'Okay.'

'Everyone the peace industry dismissed – everyone who found another job – is in a holding cell at headquarters. All the homeless went to Portland Yard.'

'Is that somewhere out of town?'

'It's a landfill site.'

'Oh.' I'm not sure what to say, but I can guess what's coming.

'I've seen it named a few times before. I always thought it was a workfare thing – that they were sorting refuse or something – but this many, all at once…'

The lift door pings open down the hall. Forensics will be setting up soon.

'Well,' Burford starts to make his way towards the door. 'I think we can give up on getting anything out of those informants.'

I take one last look at the open window, at the desk hastily moved back into place. It's more than we've had to go on so far, but still I'm not sure what headquarters expected us to get out of it.

When we get back to the lift, there's a technician in front of the doors moving several large trolleys of equipment through the hall.

'Sorry,' she says. 'Just sent it down for the next lot. You're welcome to wait, but it could be a while.'

'We'll take the stairs,' says Burford. I'm not so sure, but if it keeps Cowell from breathing down our necks then I guess it's worthwhile. He pushes open a door nearby.

'Over there,' says the technician, pointing to the end of the hall.

'Thanks,' says Burford. The door he opened was just another office. It snaps shut the moment he takes his hand away, forced by a strong breeze.

The sound reminds me of my dream. Of being pinned in the meeting room at headquarters. Of the dog, the rat, the cable in the street.

Burford moves towards the stairwell.

'Wait!' I say, before I'm even really sure why I'm saying it. It didn't happen. It was only a dream. But still, some part of my mind connects those ideas: the sniper and the rat, the sniper and the dog.

'What is it?'

I'm asking myself the same question. I push open the door, and that's when it hits me.

'Why is this window open?' I ask.

Burford joins me and stares at it. I can tell he's thinking the same thing.

'This whole floor is to let,' I continue. 'Everything else is sealed up, so why is this window open?' It's a big window. Unlike the other one – that the sniper had to force, could only reach by standing on a desk – this one swings out sideways, the opening reaching down almost to waist height.

Burford approaches it, holds his hand out in the mist of rain. 'The carpet's barely wet. It's not been open long.'

I step into the room. Down the road, the crime scene tent is obscured by another building.

Burford sees it too. 'No clear shot,' he says. 'That's why they forced the other window.'

For an instant, this makes sense to me. But then, 'What difference would it make? The constable was on foot. They might have come back into view, or another might have appeared. Is the sniper really targeting specific individuals?'

'Or was there some other reason they couldn't shoot from here?'

The dog. The rat. The blinding shock.

'Is there a power outlet in here?' I ask.

Burford ducks down. 'Under the desk.'

'It's a long way from that window.'

His eyes widen. He runs from the room. I hear the door to the other office bang against the wall.

A moment later, he's back again, radio pressed against his face. 'Get Cowell. Get me Cowell. I don't care who he's talking to! The sniper's modified the weapon. They're using mains power.'

He pulls the swivel chair from the desk and slumps down in it, to my alarm.

'This is a crime scene now,' I say. 'We have to—'

'I thought of this.' He sits with his elbow on the desk, his forehead on his palm. 'The innovation industry told me it couldn't be done.

The power supplies were too specialised. The parts were too heavily controlled. The design was too well guarded. I don't know why I believed them.'

'It's not your fault.'

'But I could have done better. If I'm going to change anything, I have to do better.'

He sits for a while. Long enough that I'm just about to say something when he speaks up again.

'How did you know?'

'I…' It's not a question I was expecting. 'I didn't. At least, I don't think I did. But with both windows open, I thought…' I realise it's no good trying to explain about the room. It wasn't the room that told me. 'Ever since I started sleeping, I've been going through this same dream. Over and over again. It's always a little different, but every time there's electricity. I think that's what made me think of it.' It's only when I come to say it that I realise what I mean. 'There's always electricity. It's the electricity that kills.'

***

The gun is lighter than you'd think. The barrel is a fluoropolymer – high heat-resistance, low friction – with vents cut between the electromagnetic coils spaced along its length. Near the stock they're close together, to coax the projectile into motion, to overcome its inertia. Towards the muzzle they grow gradually farther apart, to raise its velocity just short of the speed of sound. I slot a bullet into the breech and raise the weapon to my shoulder, finding the place where the sight's lens reveals its image to my eye. It is the office of Superintendent Cowell. I position the reticle over his back and pull the trigger. There's barely any recoil, the rain the only sound.

I wake to raindrops on my window, and a ringing phone.

'We have to end this,' says Burford, as we drive to the site of the latest shooting. 'We won't catch the killer by locking down buildings. We won't learn their identity through industry reports. We might spot them on surveillance footage or stumble over the stashed gun or have some citizen catch them in the act, but who knows how long that could take. We have to do something. We have to be the ones to act.'

He's waiting for me to say something, to come up with some idea, but I'm all out.

'What does the sniper want?' he asks. I'm increasingly convinced that there's no answer.

'Chaos. Or maybe revenge. Or nothing. Maybe there's no reason at all.'

'We'd better hope there is. Otherwise there's no telling where they'll strike next.'

'What if Cowell's right?' I ask. 'What if the target isn't the people they're shooting at? What if the real plan is to keep the security industry off the streets, make us stick inside, rely on armoured vans? That was why he wouldn't share the information. That was why he wouldn't order ballistic vests.'

'If the plan is to keep us off the street,' says Burford, 'then it's doing less than nothing. I still don't agree with Cowell, but you've got to hand it to him: his plan worked. He set out to avoid a panic and he's done a hell of a job. If we caught this guy today, half the industry wouldn't know we'd been looking for him. The other half wouldn't know why.'

'Do you think the sniper realises that?'

'Hard to say. Might not realise, might not care. Whoever we're dealing with is disciplined, persistent. They've been doing this for weeks now. A few weeks more and word might start to get around. If that happens, Cowell's plan might do more harm than good. The rumours would probably be worse than the reality. Perhaps the sniper's counting on that. Or perhaps it makes no difference at all. Either way, it doesn't tell us which building he's in.'

Just then, something does come to me. 'Maybe we don't need to know the building. Maybe we only need to know the block.'

He glances at me.

'Like you say, we're getting nowhere trying to respond to these attacks. But what if we...' As I'm forced to select a word, it occurs to me that there are no good options. 'What if we prompt one?'

I wait for him to object to the idea.

Instead he just asks: 'How?'

'If the killer doesn't care whether or not the attacks generate a response, we'll have very little influence. But what if they do? What if they are trying to cause a panic and they're already frustrated by the lack of results?'

'Yeah? What if they are?'

'If we offered a better target then we'd at least know where they'd be.'

'I thought that was probably where you were going with this. The idea had occurred to me as well, but that's going to be a tough one to pitch to anybody higher up.'

We're at the scene. Burford stops the car and we begin to put on our rain gear before setting off towards the familiar crime scene tent.

'Let's just hope it doesn't come to that,' he says, before snapping his mask over his face.

We examine the scene. There's no blood spatter, no open window, no evidence of any kind. Electricity usage in the surrounding buildings reveals nothing conclusive. The body is the only indication the sniper was ever near.

***

'How do you know you can draw the sniper into the open?'

Cowell's not as strongly opposed to the idea as we thought he would be, though he's still quite sceptical overall.

'We don't,' admits Burford, 'and it might not. We're working on the same assumption as you: that these attacks were supposed to reduce our effectiveness as an industry, and that so far they haven't. If that's the case, we might be able to lure them to a specific location by presenting a situation in which the attack would receive significant media coverage.'

'The killer hasn't taken any risks,' I put in. 'Most likely they won't. We've yet to determine the site of more than half the shootings: the odds of a response team catching them during the immediate aftermath are extremely slim. A trap like this could be our only chance.'

***

It isn't raining, the day we finally set the trap. I can't decide if that will work in our favour, or if it risks putting the sniper off. I hope it won't make a difference either way: if all goes to plan, there'll be no more victims today.

Cowell's stand-in will give a speech in the open, airy foyer of the city hall, ostensibly broadcast live across the nation: the perfect time and the perfect target. What the killer doesn't know is that the speech has been replaced with a recording, and the windowpanes with forty millimetres of transparent ceramic. Only three buildings have a view through those windows, and we've got teams moving in already. By the time the stand-in arrives, we'll have the whole place surrounded.

'We're nearly there,' reports Burford, over the radio. 'Any activity?'

'The street's empty,' I reply. 'Everything's cordoned off: if the sniper's here, they've already taken position.'

'No sign of anyone in the windows overhead?'

'Yeah. All over the place.' It takes a conscious effort not to look up, not to reveal that I'm aware of the threat, not to make myself a target. 'The event's drawing a fair bit more attention than anticipated. There are a lot of spectators up there.'

Burford mutters something deeply unprofessional away from the mouthpiece. 'I'm surprised Cowell's stunt is actually drawing a crowd,' he says, once he's composed himself, 'but it can't be helped. All the more reason to make sure we—'

There's a sudden pop. The signal cuts out.

'Burford?' I check the radio, not sure if the noise came from his mouthpiece or my speaker. It seems fine. 'Burford, you still there?'

There's a considerable wait. Or perhaps only a few seconds. I hear nothing on the radio, but there are shouts from down the street.

'He's low,' comes Burford's voice at last. 'First floor, maybe second. Building opposite the car.'

'How do you know?'

But the answer never comes, and I already know it.

I contact headquarters as I run into the street: 'Cut the power to the block. Do it now.'

We've been ready for this. But still, there's a good half minute

100

before the lights go out: more than long enough to charge the gun for a second shot.

As if on cue, I hear it.

There's no boom, no sudden crack of gunfire. Just the dull, amorphous noise of one object connecting with another at tremendous speed.

I come to where the car lies in the road, engine running, one tyre resting on the curb. The bulletproof glass in the front left window is frosted white with fractures. I can't make out the place it's been perforated, but I know the hole is there. And I know somewhere, there's another.

One of the response teams is already on site. Here, hugging the wall, we're reasonably safe. Inside, I can't be so sure.

'We were just there when it happened,' explains an officer with a ballistic shield. 'We've covered all the entrances: they won't get out.'

'Was it this building?' I ask. 'Are you absolutely sure?'

But the car confirms it: the rear window has been shattered too, this shot aimed at Cowell's lookalike sitting in the back. The first would have been made while the vehicle was moving, the second once it had rolled to a halt. From where I'm standing, the bullet hole lines up almost perfectly with the back seat.

'Get an ambulance in,' I add, frustrated that it hasn't already happened and ashamed I didn't make the call myself.

'But the sniper—'

'He's got one shot, if that. He won't waste it on a paramedic.' If I'm honest with myself, I'm not so sure – there's no guarantee the coilgun is the only weapon he has – but Burford deserves a chance and I'm willing to take one.

There's chatter on the radio. I can't make out the words but the tone is sharp, almost frantic. The officer puts a hand to his ear as he listens.

'We're going in,' he says. 'You call it.'

So I do.

But the ambulance takes a long time to arrive.

I begin to pace along the wide front of the building. There are no shouts, no shots, but I do hear a sudden thud from the alley down the side. I approach the source of the sound.

There is a cable in the street.

I step forward numbly, expecting to find a dog, a rat, but the alley holds neither. I expect to hear my watch alarm, or feel Burford shaking me awake, but I do not wake at all. There really is a cable. One end has the sort of plug that might fit the coffee machine in the meeting room at headquarters. The other has only frayed wires. A wall plug lies in the gutter nearby.

There is a small window open on the second floor.

The cable might have reached almost to the ground.

'The sniper's left the building,' I announce into the radio. 'They're...'

But I don't know where they are now. All I know is that they can't have passed me.

I rush to the other end of the alley and find myself immediately caught up in a sudden bustle of activity. Here, out of view of the windows overlooking the scene, our forces are arranged. The road is open, exposed. I glance around, but can see nobody not in uniform, nobody passing by.

I run to the first door I find, then – remembering how Ringwald burst out at me before – draw my revolver and slowly push my way through.

The room is dark. A sort of half-basement – the only windows are small, set just below the ceiling, and all the lights are out. I consider turning on my torch, but I'm reluctant to do anything that would give away my presence. Peering through the gloom, I step farther inside.

This place is a sweatshop of some kind. There are sewing machines, tools. A desk strewn with leatherwork sits against the wall, scissors resting on a sheet of hide. A rack of knives and awls stands nearby. I thumb the hammer of the revolver.

The soft click echoes through the room.

There's a crash from nearby – far closer than I could have anticipated. I fire, and the muzzle flash reveals a flicker of movement darting for the next room.

'Stop!' I shout. 'Stay where you are!'

My ears are ringing, but I follow the sound of shoes slapping against the concrete, straining to listen past the commotion outside. There's another crash ahead. I spot a trolley overturned in the corridor, try to vault it, and completely misjudge the distance. My heel catches the far end of the trolley and I fall sprawling to the ground.

I hear a door rattle ahead and to my left, feel the follow-up kick hit the wood and travel through the floor. As I struggle back to my feet, a figure dashes left to right past the end of the hall.

'You're surrounded!' I yell, not sure if it's true. The response teams are certainly closing in: there are flashlights in the hall behind me.

I stumble forward, round the corner, bring the pistol up.

'Get on the ground now!'

He's halfway through the door, rifle clutched tight to his chest. At first I can't tell if he's trying to conceal it or just clinging on for comfort. Then he turns, and I know for sure.

He is a child.

'Put it down.' I lower the revolver. 'Just—'

There's a buzz of gunfire from outside. He falls without a sound.

***

'Well,' sighs Superintendent Cowell, 'that certainly didn't go to plan.'

I wait for him to continue while he puffs on his cigarette.

'But still: it's all over now. And you've certainly earned your promotion.' He looks at me. 'Inspector Burford would be proud to have you as his successor, you know.'

'Yes,' I manage. With the preparation involved in setting our trap, I haven't slept for days. I don't plan to again if I can help it.

'I have to keep up appearances – the industry must remain strong if it is to maintain order – but I can't afford to repeat mistakes. You and Burford showed insight into this case that I perhaps didn't fully appreciate. With hindsight, things could have been handled differently from the start. If you choose to continue his work, I'll see that you're supported along the way. You'll have the opportunity to advise the entire department. Someday perhaps the entire industry.'

'Actually,' I say, 'I think I'd like to have my old job back.'

'Are you sure?' he asks. His tone, his posture, demand I reconsider.

'I'm certain.'

'The industry needs agents like you. If you can—'

'If you're serious about taking my advice, take it now: I can't help you with that.'

'Oh.' He stops.

I can see that I've worked him into a corner.

'Well then,' he says at last. 'I suppose I have asked enough of you. Besides – as I say – it's all over now.'

There's no way one child could have captured that gun. No way he could have reconfigured it on his own. There are a million reasons why we completely overlooked him, but none of them hold without someone supporting him behind the scenes. Even Cowell should see that, but he's tired. We're both so tired.

'Yes,' I say. 'It's all over.'

***

It's getting towards five in the morning as I reach the noodle bar. The delivery system feels odd yet familiar above my sternum and beneath my skin. There's already someone being served. They press their thumb to the reader and pay without incident. They take their bowl and carry it blearily over to a table.

I step up to the kiosk.

The cook smiles: 'Red or blue?'

Patrons

365tomorrows
Caspar Addyman
Helen Adlam
Janice Alexander
Coral Ann Howells
Sandra Armor
Jessica Augustsson
James Aylett
Paul Ayres
Paul Bailey
Duncan Bailey
Jason Ballinger
Amala Balraj
Jo Bellamy
Barbara Berrington
Barry Blackburn
Adrian Blamires
Veronica Botto
Mark Bowsher
Kevin Bragg
Phil Breach
Stephanie Bretherton
Neal Brophy
Stephen Brown
Eric Brunel
Jason Buck
Amelia Bull
Gemma Burford
Tanvir Bush
Janice Butler
Scott Byrne-Fraser
Sara Cannon

Piers Cardon
Bernise Carolino
Anthony Carrick
Alex Carter
Cecily Casey
Craig Chalmers
Elaine Chambers
Leon Chatterton
Peter Chilcott
Christine Clark
Joe Clark
Catherine Clark
David Cochrane
Stevyn Colgan
Melusine Colwell
Charlotte Comley
Jack Connell
Dave Cooper
James Coote
Tamsen Courtenay
Sarah Craig
Dan Craig
Jonathan Craig
Stephen Craig
Jordan Craig
Philip Craig
James Craig Paterson
Ele Craker
Nick Davey
Jean & Murray Davidson
Marc Denton
G. Deyke
Kris Dikeman
Claire Dyer
David Eadsforth
James Ellis

Barbara Evans
Brett Evans
Jordan Dean Ezekude
Maggie Farran
Stuart Ffoulkes
Lauren Filby
Paul Fisher
Rosamund Fleming
Anita Foxall
Adam Fransella
Donald Fraser
Nick French
Sharon Fuller
Clare Gibson
Sarah M Gillis
Jess Gofton
Ian Goldberg
M.R. Graham
Thomas Grainger
Catherine Griffin
James Griffiths
Stuart Hadley
Faye Hammill
Andrea Harman
Maximilian Hawker
Liam Hayes
Rachael Hemsley
Judith Heneghan
David Henley
Karen Hercock
Rob Hicks
Brian Hooper
Mary Horlock
Annadel Horner
Kim Howard
Dave Hubble

Aida Hudson
Vera Hughes
David Hutchison
Silke Hutt
Emma Inskip
Johari Ismail
April Ivy
L J
Oli Jacobs
Margaret Jennings
Marjorie Johns
Reina Johnson
Noora "WindySilver" Jokela
Joey Jones
Ziggi Kaiser
Theo Karner
Katt
Elena Kaufman
Sam Kay
Calum Kerr
Claire Kerry
Dan Kieran
Patrick Kincaid
Gary Kings
Shona Kinsella
David Knill
Jay Knioum
Phoebe Knowles
Chris Knowles
Katie Knowles
Laura Knowles
Alison Knowles
Linda Knowles
Peter Knowles
Nadia Kuftinoff
Christine Lawrence

Ewan Lawrie
Jason Le Page
Stephen Leach
Chris Limb
Georgina Lippiett
Amy Lord
Simon Lucy
Anna Lyaruu
Ermis Madikopoulos
Andy Marsh
Jessica Martin
Marilyn Masters
Rob May
Phil McArthur
Jerry McDonnell
Scott McElney
Craig McEwan
Flora Eilidh McNeil
Margo Milne
Eileen Misselbrook
John Mitchinson
Stephen Mizen
Diego Montoyer
Shannon Morphew
Tara Morrigan
Edward Mynors
Carlo Navato
Bethany Neal
Margaret Negus
Jim Niemann
Daniel Nother
Sara O'Connor
Jan O'Malley
John-Michael O'Sullivan
Par Olsson
Sophie Osborne

Polly Owen
Scott Pack
Jezz Palmer
Jane Parker
Nico Payne
Alanna Petty
Justin Pollard
Lawrence Pretty
Summer Quigley
Cat Randle
Alex Rawlings
Michael J. Ritchie
Fiona Roberts
Sue Rose
Patricia Rougier
Mollie Russell
Russellmarkolson Russellmarkolson
Mark Rutter
Carmel Ryan
Helen & Richard Salsbury
Graeme Sandford
Angelia Saplan
Ste Sharp
Sue Sharpe
Lynn Sheil
Gillian Shilson
Matt Simpson
Ian Skewis
Niall Slater
Keith Sleight
Susan Smith
Sallie Smith
Matthew Smith
Sara C. Snider
Ali Sparkes
Joshua Sparks

Andrea Speed
Janice Staines
Simon Stanley
Pat Statham
Peter Statham
Andy Steele
Adrian Stent
Karen Stephen
Tim Stevenson
Simon Stickland
Tabatha Stirling
Justin Strain
Sarah Sutcliffe
Carrie Swille
Ricky Tart
Sally Tay
Annie Taylor Evans
Andrew Tees
Laura Thompson
Donna Thompson
Brian Thompson
Tony Tibbenham
James Timpson
Mark Todd
Rosalind Toliver
Paul Tompsett
Alexandra Turney
Joris van Dorp
Vijay Varman
Sharon Vennall
Dawn Vickerstaff
Daniel Wache
Karen Walton
May Wang
Benjamin Warburg
Cindy Warburg

Tristan Warner-Smith
Julie Warren
Stuart Watt
Cara Weston
Alex Wetter
Laura Wheeler
Mary Whitehouse
Jason Whittle
Helen Williams
Andrea Wilson
BD Wilson
Joe Wright
Jenny Wright
Julian Wright
Amber Wright
Juan Zapata
Christof Zottel Bojanowski